Though he became interested in writing at a young age, the author didn't act on it until he learned at 59 that he was adopted. Two wars and a career in government gave him much to write about. He also credits an English course that he completed in college as a young man.

This book would never have appeared on paper were it not for the inspiration provided by Frank Russ.

My wife Nonie has also kept me going after many rejections. Her never-give-up spirit has been invaluable.

Frank A. Perdue

TIME OF DEATH

AUSTIN MACAULEY PUBLISHERS™

LONDON • CAMBRIDGE • NEW YORK • SHARJAH

Ordering Information:
Quantity sales: special discounts are available on quantity purchases by corporations, associations, and others. For details, contact the publisher at the address below.

Publisher's Cataloguing-in-Publication data
Perdue, Frank A.
Time of Death

ISBN 9781645759133 (Paperback)
ISBN 9781645759294 (Hardback)
ISBN 9781645759300 (ePub e-book)

Library of Congress Control Number: 2020914328

www.austinmacauley.com/us

First Published (2020)
Austin Macauley Publishers LLC
40 Wall Street, 28th Floor
New York, NY 10005
USA

mail-usa@austinmacauley.com
+1 (646) 5125767

Both Google and Wikipedia have been invaluable in providing geographical and historical information not readily available elsewhere.

This is the strange story of Private Alex O'Bannion, USMC. By late 1942, he was listed as missing in action on Guadalcanal in the Solomon Islands. He'd been an advance scout for his battalion, as they were moving toward an enemy airfield deemed strategic. The mission was to kill or drive off the island the entire enemy force, so as to occupy and utilize the airfield as a base to protect Australian and American interests in the entire Southwestern Pacific.

O'Bannion was about a quarter mile ahead of the main force on its right flank when he disappeared. Had he been killed or wounded, his body should have been recovered, but by the time the battalion reached the airfield and the battle was enjoined, O'Bannion was nowhere to be found. There was speculation of course that he'd been captured or, God forbid, that he'd gone over to the enemy, or even deserted. That last option didn't seem likely however, for where would he go?

There'd been a strong wind that morning from an advancing storm, and with the rustling of the huge palm trees, no one heard a shot. In fact, by the time the force arrived at the point where the Marine should have been, it became eerily quiet there in the jungle. He was just gone. By 1946 when all the prisoners had been repatriated and

O'Bannion wasn't among them, he was still listed as missing but presumed dead.

Back in the States, life went on. Emily O'Bannion, who had been married to Alex O'Bannion, had him officially declared dead by court decree. She married his twin brother Alan, after what she considered a reasonable time of mourning. The two boys had been inseparable as kids and even looked alike, if you discount the broken unset nose of the missing, now officially dead Marine. So it wasn't much of a reach for the outwardly heartbroken widow to recover rapidly, and even once in a while, late at night, to imagine her first husband had actually come home to her.

At first, Jack and Rose O'Bannion, the parents of Alex and Alan, along with a 12-year-old daughter Gloria, refused to believe their eldest child was dead. They hadn't seen a body or had a memorial. Jack himself had been in the Corps in the First World War. He thought that might give him some leverage with the War Department to find out what had happened. They drove from their home in Chicago to Washington, D.C. in their prewar Ford coupe after the war ended to check official government records or find someone who knew something. Failing to change history as recorded by the Marine Corps, they learned Alex's commanding officer had a residence in a nearby town, so they went there. Finding Lieutenant Oliver West at home in Alexandria, Virginia, they were distressed to learn nothing more than what was in the official record. They were informed that, when the squad advanced to where Private O'Bannion should have been, they found nothing. It was as if the Marine had vanished into oblivion. The lean, wiry, 20-year-old, third-generation Irish-American with wavy blonde hair and a cowlick, who had looked like he stepped out of a Norman Rockwell painting before enlisting…had everything to live for…until he seemed to have disappeared into thin air. They were told by the lieutenant that, as his squad advanced toward their objective, an airport manned by the Japanese, they looked for him. He had not responded to calls on his walkie-talkie for nearly an hour since his last report, which indicated no contact with the enemy. His counterpart, on the other side of the battalion, had been reporting regularly.

The jungle was rather thick as they plodded through, with palm fronds covering the earth. A thorough search wasn't possible because of the wartime situation, but after the fierce battle with the Japs at the airfield, in which all of the enemy combatants were either killed, captured, or ran off, hoping to fight another day, his squad went back to where they felt O'Bannion had been when he disappeared. His body was not found, nor was there any evidence the Marine had ever been there.

1

In the normal scheme of things, Mary wouldn't have been home to answer the door that day when someone knocked. She certainly wouldn't have heard the sound as someone tried the knob. The door would have been locked, as usual, and short of breaking it down, whoever was outside would surely have turned away, and Mary Abrams would never have known someone came to her home, anxious to get inside.

But she was home, and she did hear. She'd had a persistent cold for the past week, and this one day, she decided not to go to work. She was watching *Search for Tomorrow* on the television. It had taken her a while to find the right station because she didn't watch much TV. Finally finding CBS, she settled back on her comfortable brown sofa to watch.

It was a first for Mary. The diminutive redhead had never listened to or watched a soap opera in her life. Her friend Ida had been insistent, however, assuring her that if she was sick and had nothing else to do, she would enjoy that gripping, though drawn-out drama.

True, Mary was only 19 and there were many things she hadn't experienced, but she decided what the heck, it wouldn't shorten her life.

Mary Abrams was very independent. Hadn't she left her family in Indianapolis, Indiana to pursue a career when most girls her age were looking for husbands? The youngest daughter of a Jewish family, she wanted to experience life in a big city. She chose Chicago because she didn't have bus fare all the way to New York, after saving for an apartment.

Mary might never have gone to the windy city at all if her boyfriend Jerry Ginsberg had taken the hint, and asked her to marry him. She met him at a Shabbat service one weekend. He was the same age as her, and she'd seen him at school, before she dropped out, but had not talked to him.

She wasn't really in love with the tall freshman college basketball player, and she only came up to his chest, which was a detriment. They looked like Mutt and Jeff on those few times he would take her out, usually to a movie. Still, she watched as all her girlfriends from high school married. She was tired of being a bridesmaid, and would have gone through with it, had he asked. Instead, he broke up with her. She was surprised when she wasn't devastated at all… Just the opposite, in fact. She was so relieved; she bought her ticket to Chicago that day. Marriage would have to wait.

She found a job as a clerk in Woolworth's right away, almost before she found an apartment. It was the same day. She was lucky in that respect though. A woman on the bus suggested she try the Alliant Arms on the south side of the city. The owner was a woman who might be sympathetic to a young girl just starting out. Mary called, and she was able to move in the same day. The young redhead would have liked to find a suitable female roommate, but that hadn't happened yet when there was a loud knocking sound at her door.

When she opened the door leading to the hall, she was surprised to see a tall man, dressed in a Marine battle dress carrying a rifle. He had a shocked look on his face. "Who the hell are you?" he asked, rather loudly, in a deep voice.

Mary stepped back quickly and tried to slam the door. The stranger was a little faster though, and he stopped the door from shutting with his left combat boot. It was too late to stop him as he pushed the door wide once again and stepped inside.

"I live here. My name is Mary Abrams. Who the hell are you?" she said as she regained her composure. She would not be intimidated. She'd escaped to Chicago to get away from that.

His voice softened somewhat as he answered, "Look, this is my apartment; at least, it's my family's, and you're not one of them. Where did you come from? Are you a friend of Gloria's?" The Marine studied her closely. He was sure he didn't know her. She couldn't have been taller than five-foot-two. He thought she was pretty, with her red hair up in a bun. Her eyes were wide with brown pupils. Her nose was just a little large for her face, but it did nothing to detract from the beauty he saw before him. Her clothes were strange, though. Instead of a suit, she had a ruffled white blouse and a plaid skirt that was far too long, covering her knees. He noticed she was barefoot, so she'd be a little taller when going out.

Mary was recovering her composure, "Who's Gloria? I don't know anybody by that name. You said this place was your family's. I don't know who lived here before so I can't help you there. When was the last time you were here?"

"I'll ask the questions if you don't mind. When did you move in?" There was once again a rough tone to his reply.

She would have none of that, "Look, it doesn't matter how long I've been here. If you look around, you'll see that these are my things here, not yours, or your mysterious family, if in fact you ever had one." She paused, watching as the man took a step closer to look inside. She too moved backward.

Since the stranger was obviously confused, she suddenly felt sorry for him. "What's your name and the name of your family?" she asked, for lack of anything else to say. She doubted it would help settle their dispute.

"My name is Alex. Alex O'Bannion." Not seeing any recognition on her face, he continued, "My mother, father, and sister were here in this apartment when I left to go overseas."

"How long have you been gone?"

"I left to go to Camp Pendleton in California right after boot camp in San Diego. Then I flew to Pearl Harbor in Hawaii. I was only there about two weeks before I boarded a troopship to head to the war zone."

"You mean Korea?"

"Why would I go to Korea? It's a Japanese stronghold."

"You must be delusional. The Japanese are our allies. We're fighting the North Korean communists. You're putting me on, right?"

"Who's putting who on? What you're saying doesn't make sense. How could we be fighting communists and the Japs at the same time? Russia is our ally, and so are the Koreans. We're fighting to free them."

Now it was Mary's turn to be confused, "Maybe that was true in the early '40s, but this is 1952!"

"Sure it is," he was unconvinced, to say the least. Yesterday, in his mind, he was slogging through the jungle, sinking in the mud, wishing he were anywhere else but on that island called Guadalcanal. He couldn't remember how he got to this woman's door or anything else about his trip back to the states. Had he been wounded? Was he unconscious? None of it made any sense. One thing he was sure of, though. This woman he was trying to stare down was bonkers. Why was she trying to convince him it was 1952?

He looked past her, at a painting on her wall. It was like a photograph. It looked like Times Square in New York City. There were what appeared to be thousands of people in the converging streets, and a huge sign above, on a building, with the words 'War over. Japs surrender' in huge letters.

2

The intruder stood his rifle up inside the apartment next to the door and looked back at Mary. He suddenly collapsed onto the linoleum floor in the entryway of the disputed apartment. The early World War Two combat helmet he'd been wearing flew off, rattling onto the hard surface before coming to rest nearly ten feet from his now still body. A trickle of blood escaped from his forehead to the floor below.

Mary was at a loss as to what to do next. It was now obvious Alex O'Bannion was no longer a threat to her. She just stood there, not four feet away from his inert body, for what seemed like five minutes, trying to collect her thoughts. She should call the police, but something stopped her. He looked so helpless lying there. She did, however, pick up his weapon and store it out of sight in her closet.

She noticed the wound and the blood which was drying near his scalp. She went into the bathroom, wet a washcloth with warm water, and, when she returned, gently wiped the blood from his head. It didn't occur to her to clean the floor at that time. He didn't stir. He looked peaceful for the first time since he appeared at her door. His short-cut blonde hair was tousled slightly, but there was a hint of a part on his left side. She noticed right away that his nose had been broken. It was slightly crooked, but it hardly detracted from his obviously rugged good looks. His jaw was square, and he had a dimple right in the middle of it. His eyes were closed, but she imagined him with brown eyes just like hers. He must be over six feet, she thought to herself, remembering him standing there earlier. His shoulders had been broad, almost filling the doorway, and she was reminded of the posters she'd seen of fighting men outside the recruiting station she had to pass on her way to work.

Mary made a decision that, in light of what happened later, had to be the worst ever. There was no way she could move his body by herself so she went next door to enlist help.

Jim Denton had lived there ever since Mary moved into the adjacent apartment nearly a year earlier. In fact, he tried to make a date with her the first time he saw her in the hall. He was a nice enough guy, but he was too old for her. She didn't know for sure but he was probably in his thirties. He even had some gray on the side of his light brown hair. It was hardly noticeable, but it was there.

When she pushed his doorbell button, he answered almost immediately. It was as if he was standing in his vestibule just waiting for someone to come.

"Hi, kid," he greeted her with a smile.

He just wants to show me his white teeth, she thought before replying, "Why do you call me kid? I'm at least two thirds as old as you."

"Oh, that hurts, but I'll let it go because you're so pretty. How can I help you?"

"I have a small problem. There's a Marine passed out on my floor, and I can't move him."

"Sure there is," he answered in a sarcastic tone. Then when he saw her deadpan features, he continued, "For real?"

"I know it sounds crazy, but he just showed up at my door telling me it was his apartment."

"Okay, let me get my shoes on."

As he started for what must be his closet, she noticed he was in his stocking feet.

When they reached the entryway to her place, he saw that the door was ajar. He looked at her questioningly, and she answered, "I panicked when he collapsed. I wasn't worried about the door."

He pushed it open, expecting the man's body to be in the way. It swung wide, unrestricted.

"He's gone!" Mary exclaimed. At first, she thought she had dreamt the whole thing, but then she saw the combat helmet on her carpet, maybe six feet away, and the blood on the floor where he had fallen. She rushed to her closet where she had stored the Marine's rifle. It was still there. Thinking maybe he had made it to the bedroom himself, she checked there, to no avail. He was nowhere to be seen. Surprisingly, rather than relief, she felt a little sad. Maybe she would never see him again.

"Wait here," she told Jim Denton, as she rushed out and down the hall to the stairway. She practically ran down the steps and out the door. Looking both ways, there were many people on the street. She wondered where they all came from, and if something was going on, she didn't know about. Then she realized workers were coming home from work at that time of day, and that she would be one of them, had she not taken the day off. Knowing the Marine would be easy to pick out among even a crowd, she ran to the corner, apologizing to people she bumped into as she went. At the intersection, she looked every way but didn't see him. Much slower now, she walked dejectedly back to her apartment.

Her neighbor Jim met her at the stairs. "No luck?" he asked.

"No. He's gone."

"You don't even know the guy, do you?" Then he asked the obvious question, "So why do you care?"

She thought for a second before answering, "I don't think he has any money, and he can't just go walking around the city in his uniform. People will think he's crazy. They may even lock him up."

"Why do you care? You just met him, right?"

Again, she reflected before she replied, "I don't know. He just looks so lost."

"What's he doing in uniform anyway? Did he just come from Korea? I bet if the military knew he was walking around like that, they'd lock him up in a hurry." It made sense to Denton.

Mary looked at him. He wasn't as tall as her stranger, nor as handsome. He had longer hair, which she didn't like. She preferred the short clean-cut look worn by soldiers, which reminded her… "Why aren't you in Korea?" she asked, out of curiosity.

"I have flat feet. I'm 4F."

It wasn't like her to be rude, so she thanked him for his help, even though it wasn't needed as it turned out. Then she walked to her apartment door. Looking back, he had taken the hint and was himself retreating to his own place.

Suddenly Mary felt very tired, and she went into her bedroom, stripped down to her panties and bra, and fell on her four-poster bed. She wouldn't fall asleep for a few hours though, as her thoughts were full of the man she had just met, and just as quickly lost.

3

Mary awoke to a persistent loud banging sound. At first, she was sure it was a giant woodpecker outside her window as she fought to remain asleep. When the doorbell rang four or five times, however, sleep was out of the question.

She threw on a long robe that was conveniently hanging on a hook outside her closet, turned on her bedroom light, and headed out toward her entryway. *It must be Jim*, she thought, and she prepared to lay into him for disturbing her at such an hour. She glanced at her watch which she had forgotten to remove before collapsing on her bed. It was just after midnight.

All thought of chastisement left her as she realized it was the man who had identified himself as Alex O'Bannion who had awoken her. "What are you doing here?" she asked as a smile brushed her countenance.

"I had nowhere else to go," the Marine, still in uniform, answered. A sheepish look took over as he stated, "I have no money."

"So what have you been doing," she glanced back at her watch, "in the hours since you left?" It was crazy. She was relieved to see him, even though they had just met, and the circumstances were weird, to say the least.

He answered without faltering, "Just walking. I went to the YMCA because I know they used to have beds available, but they cost a buck and a half a night, and as I said, I don't have even that much, so I looked for a place on the street where I could rest."

"You didn't find one?" she questioned.

"Actually I did. But then a cop came nearby, and I realized how I must look," he gestured with both hands to his body. "So I got out of there. Then I came here. I've been ringing and pounding for some time now."

"I know," she said, but strangely the smile remained. "Won't you come in?"

Her formality sounded a little strange to him, but he didn't hesitate as he went directly to one of her chairs and sat.

"Do you have any plans?" she asked, as she moved to her couch, which faced him from across her living room. Then she realized the only light in the apartment was coming from her bedroom, so she retraced her steps to the front of the apartment where the switches were. Soon the room was bathed in light. As she passed him, she glanced at his forehead. There was still a small cut at his scalp line with a little dried blood, but it didn't seem to bother him. She didn't think he'd noticed.

"I'd like to find out what happened to my mother and father, and my brother and sister." For some reason, he failed to mention his wife. "But I can't go chasing about town looking like this," he gestured toward his uniform once again. "I'll need a job so I can afford civvies," the dejected look reappeared on his face, "but who's going to hire me looking like this? It's more likely they would call the cops."

Somehow, they both knew he would be dependent on her for help. "What did you do before the war, I mean back in the '40s?" she realized she knew almost nothing about this man who had all of a sudden come into her life, twice.

"I'm afraid that won't help. I was a second-year student in college."

"What were you studying?" she looked exasperated as if to say, "Come on, you've got to help me here."

"I was still working on general education. I hadn't declared a major yet." All of a sudden, he looked guilty. His wife was putting him through school to be a lawyer. She herself was clerking in an attorney's office.

"What are you thinking?"

He regained his composure. He wasn't ready to admit those particular thoughts, "I'm pretty good with my hands. Maybe I can get a job as a mechanic or a carpenter."

"Okay, what did you do in the Marines?" It hit her just as she asked, that he was still in the service as far as they knew.

"I was an infantryman. Not much call for that now."

"You should check back in with the Marine Corps. You could be AWOL."

"I'll do that, but first I need to find out what happened to my family, and where I've been for the last ten years."

"How do you plan on doing that?"

"Well, first I need to talk to the landlord or owner of this building. Maybe he or she was here when they moved out. They should have left a forwarding address."

"I beg to differ, sir. First, you need some sleep, and then proper clothes for walking the streets without being thrown in the loony bin." She bit her lip for thinking maybe that's where he belonged, along with her for believing in him. But he was cute. You could say that. There was something else. He could be a criminal wanted by the police. That would be just dandy. She would be arrested for harboring him. That didn't seem to matter as she stood and walked to her hall closet. After retrieving a blanket, she threw it at him. "Here, you can use my extra bedroom. I was going to find a roommate, of the female type, but that hasn't happened yet. The bed's not made but there's a pillow on it. All this talk is making me tired again." Then she thought of something else, "Are you hungry? I can make you a sandwich."

"I don't remember eating today, or yesterday," he answered, realizing it was after midnight. He should have said, "But I don't want to put you out," but his stomach growled at that particular moment. She heard it and immediately headed for the kitchen and the refrigerator. He did say, "Bless you," with a grin.

Something else that came to the mind of Private Alex O'Bannion, after he had eaten the sandwich Mary had made him, and as he searched for sleep in that comfortable bed he was sure he didn't deserve, was the fact that he had disappeared during wartime. If he was caught, he would surely be shot as a deserter. That was most likely the reason he tossed and turned for another hour before sleep claimed him.

4

There was a euphoria that engulfed most of the free world in 1946. The war to end all wars was over, and few knew how close they came to being enslaved by Nazi Germany and the Japanese Empire. Had the German scientists developed the atomic bomb before the men at Los Alamos, the outcome might have been different. If Japan had caught our carriers unaware when they destroyed the battleship fleet at Pearl Harbor on the island of Oahu in Hawaii, to invade the West Coast of the US, we might be speaking Japanese.

One man who was keenly aware of the cliff of doom we straddled was Captain Oliver West of the United States Marine Corps. West had survived the bloody battle for Guadalcanal and Saipan and was transferred to Washington, D.C to first receive the DSC (Distinguished Service Cross) for his heroism and leadership in the fierce struggle to take the Islands from the entrenched Japanese soldiers, and then to assume a role as advisor in the War Office, which brought his promotion to captain.

West was a very sensitive man who had been a high school teacher before the war in his hometown of Akron, Ohio. The five-foot-ten 32-year-old Caucasian with pale skin, but intense caring eyes, singled out one or two students each year for extra help and guidance. Usually, they were underprivileged kids who would need education a little more than most to survive in the capitalistic world. He continued that practice in the Marines. That's why he was so disturbed when one of his men disappeared without a trace.

When the lists of released prisoners of war were published, West requested and received copies. He studied them all, looking for a familiar name. There were none.

Oliver West knew the background of Alex O'Bannion very well. They had talked often when both were at Camp Pendleton in Southern California, and later on the troopship carrying them into battle. He knew O'Bannion was a troubled youth who had been yanked from college by the draft, choosing the Marines over the army when given the chance. Were it not such a harrowing time, he might have been given a deferment because not only was he in school, but he was also married. Had there been a child, he might have requested he be passed up.

As it was, his marriage was not going smoothly. He and Emily were outgrowing each other by the time he was called up. They'd married when they were very young when they mistook infatuation for love. He'd been a second-string shortstop on the high school baseball team. Consequently, he wouldn't play unless his team was far ahead of their opponent, or the game was out of reach in the other direction. But he rode the bus with the team and wore the uniform. Emily liked the idea of going with an athlete, even a back-up. She had known him since grammar school, and she was at the age where status was high on the list of qualifications for a boyfriend.

The two had been together through their junior and senior years, and it wasn't until just before they graduated that they sealed the deal, so to speak, by sleeping together. Emily, who was a pretty girl, and well-endowed as they say, wanted to get married, and when his freshman year of college ended, lo and behold, he asked her. He was sure he was in love with Emily. They were married right away. It was June of 1941.

At first, it worked out well, but that didn't last. She worked as a receptionist in a law office to support them. Soon, he began to feel guilty for living off her, and she came to resent the fact that he was getting a higher education at her expense.

They had moved in with his parents by the time his draft notice came in January 1942. When he headed off to boot camp at the Marine Corps Recruit Depot in San Diego, California, she was being consoled by his brother Alan. He knew they were drawing away from each other, but there didn't seem to be anything he could do.

Oliver West was such a sympathetic listener, Alex told him all that, after he was assigned to the lieutenant's squad at Camp Pendleton just up the coast from where the now Private had trained earlier.

The two didn't fraternize off the base because of their respective ranks, but West had developed a soft spot in his heart for the young Marine and decided to try to protect him from the harm that would surely come to many in his platoon. He almost felt fatherly, though there were only a few years between their ages.

After the beachhead on Guadalcanal, where they encountered almost no resistance, Major Bart Lewings—the battalion commander—told his platoon leader West to assign scouts to work their way through the jungle in advance of the larger force. Before the lieutenant could object, Alex volunteered for the job. Only one other Marine stood up, and they needed two—one for each flank—so that's how Alex came to be in the location from which he disappeared.

5

On the weekend following the day Alex O'Bannion appeared at the door of the apartment rented by Mary Abrams, the complex in South Chicago made the national news. A woman was assaulted in the apartment next door to Mary's place. Now, normally a story like that in Chicago wouldn't even make headlines locally, but in this case, it wasn't a normal occurrence. The perpetrator of the attack, to cover up his crime, had set fire to the apartment before escaping, a move that endangered a great many residents.

Mary Abrams had gone shopping earlier that day, to purchase clothes for her new roommate, one Alex O'Bannion. It was obvious he couldn't buy his own wardrobe since he would have to traipse about in battle gear from World War II. He had no other clothes. Mary didn't mind, though. Raised as the oldest of three daughters, she was used to helping those who needed assistance. In fact, it had been a necessity, since both her parents had to work to care for a family too large for a one-provider household. Her mother worked as a caretaker in a large estate. Mary felt needed then, just as now.

The fire was started in the bedroom and obviously intended to silence the victim forever. What the attempted killer didn't count on was the close proximity of the next-door apartment.

Alex smelled the smoke before actually seeing anything. He reacted quickly, perhaps because of his military training, which he perceived as a recent happening, even though it had been some ten years earlier.

He rushed next door prepared to break in, but the door was not only unlocked, it was ajar. Seeing the room before him filled with acrid smoke, he took out his handkerchief to cover his mouth and nose. He could tell the fire was coming from a room straight through the living room. He dropped to the floor and crawled into what was a bedroom. He heard a moan, and even though he couldn't see where he was going, he followed the sound he'd heard. Finding a body on the bed, that had not yet become fully engulfed in the fire, which was crawling up the opposite wall, he pulled what appeared to be a woman down onto the carpeted bedroom floor. Grabbing the collar of her blouse, he pulled her toward the room adjacent to the exit, which was still clear of flames but was filled with smoke. Staying low, he continued dragging the unconscious woman until they were out the door. He then picked her up and carried her into Mary's apartment. After depositing her on the sofa, he quickly found the fire extinguisher in Mary's apartment. Before heading back to the other apartment, he called the operator at the phone company, telling her about the fire, and giving her the apparent location. He didn't remember the address from when he had lived there earlier. He only knew about the fire extinguisher because the night before, Mary had started a small fire on the top of her stove. She had panicked and reached for the extinguisher before he rushed over and put a lid on the pan that had gotten too hot.

As he ran back to the woman's apartment, he yelled, "Fire!" as loud as he could. He heard people stirring on that floor as he went back into the smoke-filled rooms.

As it turned out, Alex couldn't do much to slow down the advancing flames, but the fire department arrived less than ten minutes later, and the firemen knocked down the flames before the fire spread from that one apartment. The ceiling was burned, however, making the place just above uninhabitable too.

When Alex returned to Mary's apartment to check on the unconscious woman, she briefly opened her eyes as he leaned over her to check for breathing. She closed them again quickly. A fireman came into the room where they were, and gently shoving a concerned Alex out of the way, he began administering to the woman. Another responder carried an oxygen tank and quickly hooked it up to the victim, seemingly allowing her to breathe easier.

At the same time Mary returned carrying a rather large package, Alex remembered he was in his skivvies. *That must be a sight for everyone*, he thought, as he hurriedly went into Mary's bedroom out of sight of all the people in her suddenly overflowing living room. Somehow, in addition to the emergency workers and firemen, there were now news people and photographers. He wondered if any of them had noticed him in the almost naked state, with all the commotion in that room.

Mary didn't immediately enter the bedroom. She was curious enough to remain in her crowded living room and flit from one responder to another, trying to piece together what had happened. When she was satisfied, she knew enough, she entered her bedroom and began laughing as she saw Alex with a sheet wrapped around his torso, crouched on the far side of her bed.

"I'm sorry I took so long," she began. "I wanted to be sure I got everything you'd need." She held up the manila-wrapped package she'd brought into her apartment.

Alex responded, now grinning himself, "It would have been nice if you'd returned an hour earlier."

"How did you happen to become involved?"

"I smelled smoke, and I completely forgot my state of undress."

Mary showed a look of concern, "They're saying in the other room that you saved that woman's life."

"She could have died, I guess."

"Now you're being overly modest. A fireman I talked to said you risked your own life going in there, and if you hadn't alerted people who live here and called in the alarm, it could have been so much worse."

Alex, in a shy fashion, didn't answer, just dropping his head in response. Mary decided to drop the conversation. Instead, she threw the package at him, saying, "Here, find something you can wear. I'll keep people out of here." Then she walked out of the room, closing the door behind her.

He had barely gotten his new Levi's on when there was a knock on the door. Alex thought that was weird. Here he was in a still strange girl's apartment, nearly naked, and she was knocking on her own door. When it opened, he realized how wrong he was. A man he didn't recognize stood there just inside the bedroom.

"My name's Blake Evans," he announced, without an apology for the disturbance. "I'm a reporter with the Sun Express." With that pronouncement, he took a step toward Alex, who was still between Mary's bed and the far wall, with only the jeans covering his lithe body.

"That's far enough," he said. "What do you want?" he emphasized the word "you."

"It would help if I knew your name," the intruder who had called himself Evans replied.

Alex looked out the window toward the street. There was a cigarette advertisement on the other side of the avenue. "Chester. My name is Joe Chester," he didn't dare use his real name, for fear of being found out and charged with desertion during wartime, a hanging or firing squad offense. He had finally realized the predicament he was in.

"Well look, Chester, you're kind of a hero. You saved that woman's life," the reporter gestured toward the other room, where some commotion was still going on. "I'd like a story, some background information from you." He continued, "Is this your apartment?"

Alex was thinking quickly now, "No. I'm just visiting my cousin."

"And what's her name? Is it Chester too?" he had produced a pad and was taking notes.

"No. Her name is Mary Abrams."

"Abrams, that's Jewish isn't it?"

"What difference does that make?"

The reporter was not taken aback. "It's just background info, so I can get a feel for the story I'm doing." He certainly didn't want to antagonize his subject at this point. "Are you a cousin by marriage? You certainly don't look like a Jew."

Alex ignored the question. The reporter didn't pursue it.

Suddenly, Alex realized the bag with all his new clothes was sitting on the bed in plain sight. It wouldn't do for this guy to know he had no clothes except those. He was trying to decide what to do when Mary came back into her bedroom.

She looked at the reporter and said as forcefully as she could, "Out, right now!" She started to say something about Alex, but he had put his left index finger across his lips, signaling for her to be quiet. She got the message and just repeated "Out!"

The reporter walked toward the door, but before leaving, he looked at Alex, who he thought was Joe, and his parting shot was, "We'll get together again. You don't know it but I'm going to make you famous."

6

Blake Evans needed a big story. The ex-Notre Dame back-up fullback wasn't used to failure. While in college and studying journalism, he'd uncovered a huge cover-up in the local city government. It wasn't something the school paper could handle, and he went instead to the big city in the state next door to pass on what he had learned. In Chicago, for use of his notes, he'd been able to extract a promise of employment from the Sun Express when he graduated the next June.

The muscular six-foot-two ex-football player was going to land on his feet after all. It had been a blow when he'd been demoted to the second string after being touted as the savior of the program when he was recruited out of Saint Ignatius High School in Des Moines, Iowa three and a half years earlier. When it became obvious a pro career was out of the picture, he turned his attention to writing.

The editor in Chicago made good his promise when he graduated, but Blake had to begin at the bottom of the ladder. He was assigned a job as an assistant to one of the sportswriters. He only got that position because he'd played at one of the most prestigious universities in the country, and the sports editor figured he might have an in at Notre Dame.

Blake Evans had been buried in that same job now for three years. His career was uneventful, to say the least, as he approached his 25th year on the planet. But things were about to change.

He'd been walking nearby when the fire engine passed heading south. He broke into a trot, and three blocks later, nearly out of breath, he spotted the truck in front of what appeared to be an apartment building. The firemen were already inside when he went in. He followed the hose up the stairs to the second floor and arrived just as the fire was extinguished. He followed a man who appeared to be the chief to the apartment next door. When questioned, he produced his credentials, and he was allowed to remain, provided he stayed out of the way.

An unconscious woman lay on the couch in the living room. Blake wouldn't be able to get anything from her for a while, if ever, and the firemen were busy, some mopping up in the other apartment, and two administering to the woman while the chief looked on.

He was standing by the front door just inside the room when an attractive reddish-haired woman walked right in. She immediately went to the fire chief and said something. Blake was too far away to hear what they were discussing. She then went to another door, which he assumed was the bedroom, and entered. He started to follow the woman when the chief turned toward him, saying, "Okay, what do you need to know?"

"Anything you can tell me. Was this woman in the fire?" he pointed in the direction of the other apartment.

"Yes. She was pulled out by a neighbor," he neglected to mention the state of undress of the man they all would come to know as Joe Chester. "He's in the bedroom there."

After a few more questions, Blake learned everything the chief knew, and it was time to interview the hero in the other room. Before he could enter, however, the other woman came out. She didn't see or hear him knock then enter her bedroom.

Back at his desk, Blake Evans realized he had a lot of work to do to piece the whole thing together. For instance, he still had to get the name of the woman. Did anyone else live in the apartment with her, and if so, why hadn't they come forward? Who set the fire in the first place, or was it an accident? The fire chief had said it looked like arson, but they wouldn't be sure until it was investigated. Finally, there was the neighbor's cousin. He'd said his name was Joe Chester, but he didn't say if he lived there in the apartment, or was just visiting. Maybe the guy was who he said, or perhaps he set the fire in the beginning. He could do a broad story from what he had, but he would need to do a lot more investigating before a follow-up.

He mapped out a preliminary article and took it to the feature editor, bypassing the sports guy. He was sure he wouldn't be admonished for jumping the chain of command since this could be a front-page bombshell. The editor was impressed, and immediately confirmed he would run it. At that point, Blake Evans hadn't the least inkling of just how large the story could be, but he was about to find out.

7

Alex O'Bannion was feeling guilty as hell. Here he was in what was basically a complete stranger's apartment and beginning to feel somewhat comfortable, while the woman who was his wife had no idea her husband had come back from the war and was in fact in the same city.

Now that he had clothes, there was no excuse not to look for her. But where would he start? He couldn't ask the police for help. He'd been evasive with them when he was questioned about the fire.

A Sergeant Helmand had searched him out while he was still in Mary's bedroom. Thankfully, he was fully dressed by that time.

"Was the woman unconscious when you found her?" he began.

"Yes."

"How did you get in after you smelled smoke?"

"The door was ajar," Alex was already beginning to tire of all the questioning. There was no way to avoid it, though. The idea he might be a suspect hadn't crossed his mind at that point.

"Was anyone else in the hallway or the woman's apartment when you entered?"

"No."

"Did you know the woman?" the detective's eyes seemed to be boring right into Alex.

"No. I'd never met her."

"How long have you lived in the apartment next door?" The questioning became more personal and went on for what seemed like an hour. Alex lied about his name as he had with the reporter. When asked if he had identification, he said he had left it at home, which was in Columbus.

"Did you drive all the way here without a license?"

"I took the bus," Alex replied quickly, perhaps too quickly.

The sergeant, who was a big man with dark eyes to go with his blue serge suit, obviously wasn't satisfied, but he ended the interrogation with, "Don't leave town, Chester. We're definitely going to want to see you again." Then, softening a little, he added, "Nice job, pulling the woman out. You obviously saved her life."

After the interview, Alex knew his story wouldn't stand up to scrutiny, and he decided he had to get out of Mary's apartment. He had no money and no identification, but he was sure at that moment, he would be arrested and charged with assault at the least if he stayed.

If he could find his wife, and maybe even his mother and father, together they could make sense of what was happening to him, and this thing that was becoming a nightmare would end.

8

An officer was stationed outside the hospital room of Judy Graves. The police weren't sure whether or not the severely burned woman was still in danger. They were taking no chances.

It was the night after Blake Evans' story hit the newsstands that she had a visitor. She had just been rolled out of surgery into her room and she was still unconscious when her father entered. He pulled up a chair next to her bed on the side opposite from where she was hooked up to machines.

Now normally no one would have been able to gain admittance to the room, but being her father, he was admitted.

At first, Vince Arrizano had no idea the woman burned in the apartment fire was his daughter. She had changed her name right after she moved out of the family compound.

There'd been a big verbal fight that day. IIis daughter, whose name was Judy Arrizano, had just found out what her father did for a living. She'd come back early from the college her family had enrolled her in, determined to quit school. A classmate had enlightened her about her father's profession. At first, she didn't believe it. The man she knew was not capable of all the vile things he was accused of. The young man had shown her an article about a missing bookmaker, where Vince Arrizano was the leading suspect. So far, they hadn't been able to prove anything.

Judy knew her father was a crude, uneducated man, but she also saw his gentle side. When her mother had fallen ill with that horrible disease, he never left her bedside, until the illness claimed her. Judy was only nine, and he had raised her after that, never denying her anything.

He had provided well for her. She had her own room, filled with various stuffed animals he had bought her over the years. It was a practice that continued into her teens.

It seemed the mansion built on the southern shore of Lake Michigan was always crowded with business associates, and even she had to call to be allowed through the gates to the property. She just thought that showed how important and rich her father was. She was very proud of him.

On the day she came home for the last time, her father met her at the French double doors leading into the vestibule.

"Why are you home?" he began, a little louder than usual.

"I quit school. I'm not going back," and she added, "no matter what you say."

"You'll do what I tell you to do. You're not 21 yet."

"I will be in April, and believe me, you don't want me here, not with what I know."

"Just what do you think you know, young lady?" He had no idea what she was getting at.

She just blurted it out, "How you got all your money!" Her voice was rising, "Who did you have to kill?" She was right in his face, "Did you kill my mother too?"

Vince's face turned red, and he slapped his daughter across her left cheek, knocking her back a couple of steps.

"What do you think this life is, a picnic? Do you think a guy like me, who never had a real bed until I was a man," and he raised his arms expansively, "could ever hope to have any of this?"

Judy began to cry, but he went on, "Maybe it's time you knew. I beat a man to death with these hands before I was your age. Yeah, and I didn't cry over it either. I spent three months in jail before I went to trial. I was released when they ruled it self-defense. But they didn't give me my three months back, or pay me for it. I made up my mind then that I would control my life, and no one would take anything from me ever again."

With an incredulous look, she ran out, saying, "You're a monster. I never want to see you again as long as I live."

He didn't follow, but he fell into a nearby sofa, his head in his hands.

That was a year earlier. She kept her promise. He hadn't heard from her at all. He'd tried to find her, to no avail. She'd obviously changed her name. He didn't know if she was even still in the city. He put out the word to all his lieutenants that there would be money in it for them if they located his daughter.

What he didn't know was that one of his bodyguards had been in touch with the woman now known as Judy Graves from the moment she stormed out. Eddie the Tuna was infatuated with Judy. He had actually helped her legally change her name and get a job in one of the townships surrounding the big city. He had also visited her at her apartment. She liked him, but he was just too close to her father, and she didn't want that kind of life.

Eddie Smythe had acquired the moniker Eddie the Tuna when the boss and a couple of other associates had gone fishing off the coast of Florida. Vince had a big one on the hook, but he had to relieve himself, so he handed the reel to his bodyguard, who promptly was pulled into the water by the dominant fish. He was lucky to survive.

Things might have gone on as they were, but Eddie slipped up one day. Vince heard him on the phone talking to someone he called Judy.

The elder Arrizano pulled him away, and as he did, the phone cord separated from the wall box, abruptly ending the call. Upon confrontation, the younger hood confessed he was indeed talking to Vince's daughter, who was his girlfriend. Enraged now, Vince pushed his open right hand into the nose of the frightened bodyguard, catapulting him back and onto the tile flooring, where Vince quickly wrapped his big hands around his throat, "Tell me where she is, or I'll kill you right here." He was out of control and would have killed him if he didn't need the information.

So Vince got what he wanted.

Not long afterward, Eddie the Tuna was found at a dumpsite in Indiana, burned almost beyond recognition. There were no clues to who killed him.

9

It wasn't exactly a new idea Oliver West had. It had been kicking around in the back of his head for a long time now; ever since he'd been pulled out of Guadalcanal back in 1942. He would have followed up on it sooner, but he didn't have either the money or the time. Then for a while, life got in the way.

From the battle for Guadalcanal, he went on to other Pacific theaters, and then to a desk in Washington, D.C. He met, courted, and married a stunning woman from Baltimore in 1944, who was working in the same building as he.

It wasn't until a man and woman from Chicago sought him out in 1946 that the idea resurfaced. Mister and Missus Jack O'Bannion needed to know what happened to their son Alex who was listed as missing in action on Guadalcanal. Of all the battles and skirmishes of the war that West had participated in, Alex O'Bannion was the only Marine under his direct command who was not accounted for. Sure he'd lost men, far too many, but they were dead. Their bodies had been recovered. They'd had proper burials, and their loved ones had closure. Not so for the O'Bannion family. They would always wonder if their beloved son had been killed that day in 1942, or if he had been captured. Even though there was no record of his ever being held prisoner by the Japanese, that didn't make it so in the minds of his caring parents, or his commander for that matter.

By 1951, Oliver West, Major USMC inactive reserve had all his ducks in a row, so to speak. His marriage was on an even keel. He and his wife Marjorie had two healthy boys, and he was the vice-president of a thriving bread company. He had a punctured eardrum, courtesy of a sniper bullet on Saipan that had grazed him. It kept him out of the Korean police action that was really a war.

The image of the young private seemed to be with him always, especially at night, even after he and his wife made love when he should have been at peace and relaxed. He remembered the eager way O'Bannion had jumped up when volunteers were needed. The man, who in many ways was still a boy, had no lack of courage.

He had heard of a group of military parents who had formed a co-op to specifically search for bodies or information about soldiers, sailors, and Marines who had been listed as MIA and were still on the list; that is, the disposition of their cases had not been resolved. The group was not sanctioned by the government, and therefore had no monetary support other than what they raised themselves. They were not deterred, however, and they were able to raise a considerable war chest.

It was determined they would begin on Oahu in the Hawaiian Islands and fan out across the Pacific in the same order the battles were fought. They would search out ex-combatants, both American and Japanese who still inhabited these locations, gleaning any information they could about the missing boys, and even in some cases girls, nurses, or women who were supporting the war on the allied side.

Oliver would have liked Marjorie to accompany him. They still treasured all their time together. It wouldn't have been practical, however. Both boys were still in school and needed at least one parent to be home when they arrived. She no longer needed to work and was happy being a homemaker.

They embarked on a cool, windy day in December 1951 from where they had assembled in Los Angeles. It would be a long flight, as jet travel had not yet arrived on that route.

Oliver spent much of his time on the DC-3 thinking about all that had happened in the five-plus years since the elder O'Bannions had walked into his home back in 1945. He wasn't much for reading magazines. It had been a shock to read of their passing not two years later. Living in another state, he shouldn't have even known about the automobile accident that took their lives, but as luck or fate would have it, the estate executor had come across his phone number in their papers and called to advise him of their demise, in case it was important somehow. He found a copy of the paper detailing the accident at the library. It saddened him, even more, to know they never had the peace that finding their son would have given them.

Technically, it was listed as a traffic accident, but in fact, they were walking their six-month-old Great Dane when they were hit. Normally, they would have been on the oncoming side of the road so they could see any danger coming. In this case, however, there was a wide sidewalk on the other side that was set back from the street almost ten feet. They should have been safe there. The driver approaching behind them, a 72-year old woman who still smoked, was reaching for the cigarette lighter in her new Cadillac when her car veered toward the curb. By the time she recovered control, she had racked up two victims. The dog was not hit and survived.

The court took pity on the old lady, sentencing her to probation, with the stipulation she does not smoke for six months. Of course, there was no way to enforce the no-smoking decree, and she quietly puffed away in the solitude of her own home. No one was surprised when she contracted lung cancer the next year. In those days, it was a death sentence.

Late in 1949, Oliver had business in Chicago, and he took a side trip to visit Alex's ex-wife and his brother, who by then were an unhappy married couple. He never got to meet them. One night, only a few months earlier, in a paranoid schizophrenic rage, Emily O'Bannion took a knife to her husband as he was sleeping. She thought he was literally a monster come to do her harm. The judge sentenced her to only two years' incarceration after she was found guilty of her husband's murder, but with extenuating circumstances, after her highly-paid lawyer convinced the jury she was a battered wife.

Instead of providing help for her condition when she was released penniless after serving only 18 months in the county jail, they allowed her to roam the streets in a mental state until she died of starvation in an alleyway in the back of a Goodwill store. There was no family left to help her. The authorities never knew she had a sister-in-law that they could have contacted.

As the aircraft circled in the pattern for landing in Honolulu, Oliver West had one last thought. In his mind, he pictured the entire O'Bannion family sitting around the dining room table, laughing and joking, without a care in the world on December 6th, 1941.

10

There was something about the man who identified himself as Joe Chester that bothered Bill Helmand. As he sat at his desk, set back in the corner of the south side station, he decided to call Columbus, Ohio to obtain background on the perceived hero, who could indeed be the attempted killer of Judy Graves.

He could wait to see if the woman regained consciousness. Maybe she could identify her attacker and save considerable police work, but that wasn't his style. Bill Helmand was a bulldog. That's why he made detective after only five years on the Chicago police force. He wasn't afraid to get his hands dirty, as long as it was legal. He was a straight shooter, as the saying goes. It had nothing to do with firearms, though he was a good marksman, scoring high when he qualified with the police .38. When he promised something, he followed through. You knew just what you were getting with Bill (Bull) Helmand.

He got the moniker in the army, trudging across France in the war. He was a squad leader who didn't know how to delegate. If a German pillbox had to be eliminated, he was the one to charge first, after ordering his men to back him up with covering fire. He was fortunate to have survived, but survive he did with nary a scratch. He would have stayed in the army, but he was denied promotion from sergeant for the very reason he got the nickname. The brass just didn't feel he was a good enough leader, because he took too many chances. He left the military in 1947, returning to his home in Chicago, where he immediately applied to the police force and was accepted. The qualities that kept him from advancing in the army were just fine for law enforcement.

This guy Chester interested him. He heard from the cop on the beat who had first encountered him that the guy was in his skivvies. Most civilians would have put their pants on, given the alarm from the safety of their own place, and then skedaddled out of the building, preserving their safety. Chester did just the opposite.

How about this scenario? He's making out with the broad, but she decides not to go through with it. He becomes furious and rapes her. Then he panics and sets fire to the place to hide his deed. Afterward, thinking she's dead, he decides to cover up the whole thing by pretending to rescue her. It could have happened that way. Yeah, he's my guy.

He picked up the phone, dialed long distance, and got the operator. She gave him the Columbus Police Station number and connected him.

"Columbus Police. This is Patrolman Jones speaking," was the answer.

"Yeah Columbus. This is Bill Helmand, a sergeant in Chicago," and he added, "Illinois," just in case the guy on the other end was from a different planet.

51

"What can I do for you, Sarge?"

"I need a trace on a suspect named Joe Chester. He said he came from there. I want to know if you have any priors on him and anything else you can tell me."

"Sure. No problem. What's your phone number over there? I should be able to track this fella down today. It's kinda quiet here right now."

"Great," and he gave the helpful guy on the other end of the line his number before hanging up.

He had gotten a call from the hospital that the Graves woman was finally awake, so he decided to head over there to check on the victim. The nurse on the case had told him she would call if the Graves woman woke up, and she had followed through.

He'd given so much thought to the suspect, it hadn't occurred to him to investigate the woman. He just assumed she was innocent in all of this. Had Helmand bothered to find out who she really was, his investigation might have taken a different direction altogether.

Traffic was heavy for a Thursday at lunch hour, and it took him over a half hour to traverse the three miles across town to the hospital. So he wasn't in the best mood when he arrived. They were working on the elevator in the lobby, and he had to walk the six flights up to the intensive care floor. He was huffing and puffing when he made it. He realized after it was too late that they had to have another elevator somewhere. They wouldn't make patients walk.

He also decided to lose some of the stomach weight he had put on since he discovered that great Italian restaurant near his home.

The officer sitting upright reading a newspaper outside the door of the private room occupied by one Judy Graves was named Oscar Snivel. He took a lot of ribbing for that at the station house. He quickly folded the paper and dropped it on the floor when the sergeant appeared at the top of the stairs a couple of doors down. He didn't come to attention, however.

"Hi, Sarge. Everything's quiet here," he announced, a little more loudly than required in the hallway where it didn't take much to produce an echo.

"Officer. How's it going?" Helmand replied.

"Good. The Graves woman had a visitor earlier, but he just left. He said he was her father, so I let him pass."

"Did he show identification?"

Snivel got a sheepish look on his face, "I guess I should have asked, huh?"

The sergeant didn't answer. He pushed the door open and entered the room. He was shocked to see Judy Graves sitting up, picking at her lunch.

11

Alex had gathered up the battle clothes he'd worn earlier and put them in a brown paper bag he'd found under the sink in her kitchen. He didn't want to carry them around, so he stored them in Mary's closet with his rifle and helmet. He was just about to leave the apartment on his way out of town when Mary walked in. "What are you doing?" she asked.

"I'm sorry, Mary. You've been swell, but I have to get out of here."

"Why? Did I do something wrong?"

He replied, "It's not you. It's me. I'm afraid I'll be arrested if I stay."

"They can't arrest you. You haven't done anything wrong."

"Yeah, but that might be hard to prove. I don't even have any identification, and it won't take them long to find out Joe Chester doesn't exist." He paused before continuing, "What if they find my uniform and put two and two together with the conclusion, I'm a deserter? I'd be in even a worse jam then."

"Have you forgotten you don't have any money?" She had intended to give him some, but he didn't know that.

He looked at her more closely than he had before. She had a little bump on the end of her nose that made it look like it was turned up slightly, but it did nothing to hide how pretty she was. Her reddish hair, parted slightly on the side on this day, curled up on the ends, and went well with her brown eyes. She wore little makeup. She didn't need it. She was about five-foot-two, which was slightly shorter than most women he'd known. She wore a pink cashmere blouse on top of a brown plaid skirt. Her shoes were a matching brown, and her socks made her look like a bobbysoxer of days gone by.

"Aren't you supposed to be at work?" he asked.

"It's my lunch hour, and I took a little extra time. It's a good thing. You might have gotten out of here without even saying goodbye."

He grinned, "I was going to leave a note."

"That's not good enough," she replied, pouting slightly. "Where will you go?" she continued.

"I thought I'd try and find my mother and father," he still wasn't prepared to admit he had a wife. He wasn't sure why. This girl who he was ready to leave behind surely didn't mean anything to him, except as a friend who had helped him when he needed it desperately.

I should just let him go, she thought. *He obviously needs to find where he belongs.* Instead, she said, "You can't just walk out of here in broad daylight," which was silly, because now that he had clothes to make him look like everyone else; he'd be perfectly safe unless he ran into a cop. She was clutching at straws because she really didn't want him to leave. *Come on. You don't know anything about this guy, except what he's told you. You have to admit the whole story is very strange. He could be a deranged psychopath for all you know. Then why am I taking his hand as these thoughts go through my head?*

"Give it at least another day, Alex. Maybe we'll think of something to get you out of this mess." His hand was warm but not clammy, and it felt good to touch him.

Come right down to it, he didn't really want to leave. He bent slightly and put his lips to her forehead, saying, "You talked me into it," adding, "but tomorrow I go."

"Sure," she replied with a smile, thinking *I'll come up with another excuse for you to stay before then.*

He thought of something else, "You'd better get used to calling me Joe if I'm going to stick around. It wouldn't do for anyone else to hear you use the name Alex where I'm concerned."

"Yes, Joe," she liked the name Alex much better, but she would do what he said.

When she had left to go back to work, Alex searched the apartment for a phone book, thinking maybe his parents were listed. Emily could be in there too for all he knew. In a way, he hoped he wouldn't find her name. They'd been at odds when he left to go to war, and he wasn't sure he wanted to repair the damage, now that he'd met Mary. It was as if he'd been a child before the war, but now he was a grown up with different needs and desires. He also knew he would have to find and confront the woman he'd married to find out how they both felt.

Though it was still midday, the apartment seemed dark and dreary when just a few minutes earlier it was alive and sparkling.

12

For lack of anything better to say, the detective—as he entered the room of Judy Graves—opened with, "I'm glad you're feeling well enough to sit up. I hear your father was just here."

"Who are you?" she responded, as she perused the man who was now standing a few feet from the foot of her bed.

"I'm sorry Miss, I sometimes forget I'm not in uniform. My name is Bill Helmand. I'm the detective assigned to your case."

"Oh. Have you found the man who attacked me?" Her voice seemed melodic and very pleasant.

He found himself staring at her. "Not yet, I'm afraid," he muttered as he regained his composure. She was very pretty. He was glad at that point the flames had not reached her face, though she was bandaged up to her chin. He was remembering he was still a bachelor. "I was hoping you could tell me who attacked you." Back to business.

"I'm afraid not, officer. He was wearing a hood. I couldn't see his face at all."

With disappointment showing in his voice, he asked, "Could you tell how tall he was?"

"He was about average, I guess, not as big as you."

"Did he force himself on you?" It was a little less direct than asking about the rape word.

"Yes. I think so, but I'm not sure," then she began to cry as if she were going through the ordeal all over again.

He was quick to try to calm her, "I'm sorry Miss Graves. I know this is hard for you, but anything you can tell me about what happened could be helpful in catching that son of a bitch."

She regained her composure somewhat, "He was very strong. I remember that."

"How was he dressed? Was he wearing work clothes? Maybe a tie?" *Come on lady, give me something*, he thought.

"He wore slacks, gray I think, and his shoes were pointed, not round at the toe like some." It was funny how she remembered that, but he had grabbed her by the hair before he threw her on her bed, and that's when she looked down and saw the shoes. Then he hit her with his fist in the face. She blacked out after that. She did remember seeing a man bending over her, but there was nothing about him she could recall, not his face, not anything.

The detective was frustrated. He was so sure she would wrap up the case for him, and now he was right back at the beginning. It seemed the only hope to break the mystery was if the FBI came back with definitive fingerprints. Then he remembered when he had asked about her father, she had avoided the question.

"What did your father have to say?"

"He was just happy I was awake," she averted the detective's eyes as she answered.

He noticed and filed that away for future reference. "That's good," he said, trying to be polite. He didn't want her to break down again. "Look, Miss, I hate to ask all these questions, but the smallest thing might help us catch the guy who tried to kill you."

"I understand. Ask away."

"Do you have any boyfriends?"

"No. Not right now," she was thinking of Eddie, who had stopped coming by, but she was sure that wasn't important, and she didn't want him to be hassled. "There's nobody." One other man had politely asked her for a date. She refused because she was with Eddie. Had that not been the case, she might have accepted. He was a nice enough looking guy. He never asked her out again, even though he lived in the same building—on the same floor, as a matter of fact.

Helmand was gathering his thoughts when a woman dressed in a blue gown entered the room. "Are you Sergeant Helmand?" she questioned, looking at him.

"Yes, I am," he answered courteously. He assumed the woman who asked the question was a hall nurse or attendant.

"There's a telephone call for you at the nurse's station."

Assuming it was important if they called him there, he thanked the woman who had delivered the message and stepped out into the hall. She followed, pointing in the direction he should go. When he got to the nurse's station, another woman dressed in the same garb handed him a phone.

"Yeah, this is Helmand," he answered, rather curtly. He didn't like to be interrupted in the middle of an interrogation.

"Sarge, the fingerprint analysis is in from the FBI."

"Yeah, so what does it say?"

"There's three or four good sets, and one of them is a new player."

"What do you mean?" the caller had Helmand's complete attention now.

"Well, the hero's prints are there, compared with the ones we lifted from him after the fire, and the girl's, of course, then there was a guy named Ed Smythe. His prints were all over the place, according to the FBI. The Feds think he may have been her boyfriend since there were so many of those prints. There were a lot of smudges identified as coming from a guy named Tony Angelo, who I think is the super of the building. The other set they pulled belong to a guy named Jim Denton. We've got nothing on him."

13

When Judy Graves' father found out where his daughter had gone, he hired a detective to keep tabs on her. He was concerned that, having been protected all her life, she might be too naïve, and get into trouble. For a while, she was fine. After a short period, however, the shadow reported Eddie the Tuna had come calling on a regular basis. Of course, he only knew the guy as Eddie because Judy would never use the nickname, and the detective wasn't privy to the fishing story. It didn't make much difference by that time, however, because the said caller was resting at the town dump.

Jim Denton had been hesitant about taking the shadow job. He wasn't hired by Vince Arrizano. Had he been approached by the big man himself there would have been no doubt. He would have taken the job, even as a courtesy without pay. He would do it for two reasons. First, he was intimidated by the mobster's status and would have been fearful for his life if he turned the job down. Second was the business side of it. He could be sure he would be retained again, should he do a good job. When he was hired, it was by a mouthpiece for the mob. The lawyer was a slick-talking, well-dressed man who offered him a good deal of money for a job that could take months to complete. It was a monetary windfall he couldn't refuse.

Jim Denton had done all right up to then, but this was a whole new ballgame. This Judy Graves must really be important to somebody.

He moved into the Alliant Arms on a Sunday. He was able to get within one floor of his target.

Judy Graves had an apartment on the second floor of the four-story building. He decided the best way to observe what was happening with her was to gain her confidence. A good way would have been to meet her when she was taking her dog for a walk. The only problem with that was she didn't have a dog. He told the super he wanted to get a little higher up in order to enjoy the skyline. Meanwhile, he spent much of his time in the lobby, pretending to read a newspaper, and drinking loads of free coffee while waiting to tail her if and when she went out. Within a month, a vacancy opened up, and he moved in two doors away from his quarry.

He quickly made the woman's acquaintance, managing to take the elevator at the same time. After introducing himself, he hit her up for a date, suggesting they meet for coffee or a drink. She naturally refused politely, telling him she was involved with someone. Denton asked his name, matter-of-factly, and she provided the information willingly.

"How long have you known this guy?" he was taking a chance, coming on a little strong, but he decided he could smooth it over should she hesitate.

She took the question in stride, however, "Nearly a year." She didn't embellish.

"Well, I don't like him," he replied, but he smiled so she would know he was joking. It would be much easier if she liked him, so he was prepared to turn on the charm.

She returned his smile and seemed to relax in his presence.

"I'll probably ask you again, you know, because you're so pretty." It was true. She was striking, and he would have been definitely interested if it didn't get in the way of business.

They bumped into each other almost every day it seemed after that. She just thought it was a coincidence. He was very helpful, even carrying her groceries in for her.

He considered making a move and stepping up the relationship. It was about that time that a body, burned beyond recognition, turned up at a city dump.

14

It was the same dream as the night before, and the night before that. He could count on waking up with his night clothes sticking to his body, and the top sheet wrapped around him at least once a week ever since he ran away, and was hidden by the natives on the island far from both his homes.

He'd grown up in the United States—East Los Angeles, to be exact. It wasn't until he was 18 that he even saw Japan. He would have been perfectly content to remain right where he was and go to college at UCLA. He'd been offered a scholarship in cross-country. He really wanted to play football, but at 130 pounds, that would have been something to see. He planned to study religion. He'd become a devout Baptist while attending church on Sundays. He talked of it often with his sweetheart Janet, a girl of mixed race. Her father was American, and her mother Japanese. She'd been attracted to the gentle boy when they were both juniors in high school.

Kyoto (Willie) Shigera was bound to his family. If his father said they would go back to his elder's place of birth, then that's what they all would do. His mother knew of her only child's desires and wanted nothing more than to fulfill them, but she wouldn't dare argue the point. They were a very traditional Japanese family, even though they were surrounded by capitalist thinking.

They boarded a freighter that took passengers along with cargo on a warm July day in 1941. The trip took nearly a month after stops in Honolulu and Guam. They arrived in the seaport of Sasebo just ahead of a typhoon. It was all they could do to find shelter before being battered by winds over 100 miles an hour. As it was, they were inundated with pelting rain and drenched to the skin before reaching the safety of a hotel, which was on a small hill, and therefore protected from the storm surge coming from the east.

Not long after they found permanent residence, Kyoto was conscripted into the army. College would have to wait, and so would his return to his intended in the U.S. After a short period of training, he was sent to the island of Guadalcanal, along with a considerable force, to help build an airfield and defend it, should the Americans come. He missed his family, but at first, life on the island wasn't so bad. He refused to consider that he might have to kill someone from the land of his birth. He was not a coward, but his deep religion prohibited him from taking another's life. That was compounded by the fact he had lived in America through his formative years. They were such a peace-loving nation, and Kyoto still considered the United States home. He had been told about Pearl Harbor, but he had not been in the invading force, thank God.

Life on the large island wasn't too bad. It was a beautiful setting that afforded spectacular sunsets on those times he could get away from his inland duties and trek to the water's edge. He often went there with his friend Ito. He was about the same age and build as Willie. They compared growing up in Japan and the United States, neither giving thought that they would soon have to kill Americans. They talked of girls, those mystical creatures that they couldn't understand. They also talked about religion. Ito was not a Buddhist. He wasn't anything really. He believed there was a higher power, but he had no idea what. They were both naïve, but happy. Maybe the war would pass them up in that idyllic setting.

After the airfield was completed, both Willie and Ito were surprised that they weren't returned to Japan or even the war zone in China. It looked like they would have to spend the Christmas of 1942 without their families.

There was no church of Willie's faith on the island, but that didn't stop him from praying in seclusion. Every night, he would seemingly wander into the dense jungle surrounding their camp near the newly constructed landing strip, and pray silently under the stars, which he perceived as heaven.

He was becoming hard under his work uniform. Weeks of lifting heavy objects had done a good job of sculpting his upper body and arms. His legs were slightly spindly, however, but they continued to hold him up. His weight had ballooned to the lofty number of 140. Of course, he had no way of knowing that. There were no scales on Guadalcanal. If there had been, they would have measured in grams and kilograms rather than the pounds and ounces Willie had been used to.

Most nights, he would fall asleep minutes after hitting his cot. There were few dreams in those days. What pictures he did create in his mind were pleasant, and many times he conjured up images of his beloved Janet. It was true, for him at least, that absence made the heart beat a little faster. As a lowly soldier, he couldn't know that destiny had chosen a path for him that would change his life forever.

15

Alex, now known as Joe, was worried. He had told Mary he would stick around for a while, because she asked him to, and because he was becoming infatuated, no matter how hard he fought against it. He had a wife, for Christ's sake. He had no right to think of another woman in those terms. But she was beautiful. *Uh oh, there I go again*, he thought.

He had not confided his predicament to another soul since he'd walked into her apartment. Consequently, there was no one else he could turn to for help. He was tied to her in that respect. He hadn't been dependent on anyone else other than the Marines since he'd reached manhood. The lieutenant had helped him, but he hadn't asked for it.

Everything was coming to a head. He had to do something, come up with a plan of attack. They had his fingerprints! Before long, the authorities would know his true identity. That Sergeant Helmand was no dummy. There would only be two choices—turn himself in, or run for his life. Running would require resources—money, a place to go. It became clear he would have to find his wife or his family. There was no other way. When Mary came home, he would tell her. He'd have to leave that night. Helmand would be camped on his doorstep in the morning. He was sure of it. Leaving town was the only option. He hoped Mary would understand. He should probably tell her he was married. He couldn't understand why he hadn't done it before.

The door opened and there she stood. The glow from the light shone from behind her through the opening, and it was as if she were an angel come to save him. He could feel his resolve to leave draining slowly from him. She was so pretty.

She was the first to speak, "Oh, thank heaven. All day I've had this terrible feeling that you'd gone." She took a step toward him.

Inadvertently, he stepped back. There was that one unsaid thing between them. He was married! He realized what he had done when he saw the bewildered look on her face. He tried to soften the blow, "I'm sorry, Mary. You startled me. I thought for just a moment an angel had entered the room."

The worried lines on her face softened and seemed to return to that place where they could not be seen. It was an awkward moment to be sure, and she tried to make light of it, "You look strange in those clothes. I think I should have let you pick them out."

He stood there, less than a room apart from her, and he looked down at himself. His Levi's had a cuff about four inches wide, and his shirt sleeves had to be rolled up to fit behind his hands. He looked like an Iowa farmer, only with bright new clothes. His shoes were the only part of his outfit that looked somewhat normal. They were of the dress variety with a store shine. He grinned, "I guess the school dance is out, huh?"

As she floated farther into her living room and took a seat on her couch, he continued, "I need to share something with you, but it will have to wait a few days. I need the answers to some questions first."

"What questions?" she seemed to have forgotten that he'd said his family was in Chicago.

"I have relatives out there somewhere. I should try to find them."

"Where will you start?" she was keenly aware he couldn't just waltz into a police station and ask for help.

"I thought I'd go to a library and check the latest census. Maybe I'll get lucky and they'll be listed there."

"That's a good idea. I'll go with you." Before he could object, she rose and waltzed into her bedroom, saying, "I need to change. Just give me a minute." Then as an afterthought, she stated, "Do you think they'll still be open? It's almost 5 pm."

He was frustrated. He needed to get the answers alone, but he didn't know how to tell her without hurting her feelings. Finally, he said, "Maybe you're right. It might be better if I go tomorrow. How about a movie instead?" She didn't answer right away, and he finally realized she must have gone into her bathroom. With the door shut, there was no way she would have heard him.

It must have been five minutes later when she finally reappeared. She'd changed into a flowing powder blue dress accentuated by dark blue high heels. Her long reddish-tinged hair was done up in a bun in the back, held by a small clip.

"That doesn't look like a library outfit to me. I'm taking you out to dinner and a movie. The research can wait until tomorrow."

She beamed. It was exactly the outcome she'd hoped for.

16

Blake Evans was about to keep his promise. He had made a grand exit from the apartment of Mary Abrams by announcing he would make the man he knew as Joe Chester famous. When he said it, he had no idea just how famous Alex O'Bannion would really become. Joe Chester was just a shmuck who was going to get his 15 minutes of fame and then fade into the sunset like so many others. But Blake on the other hand would be the fair-haired boy for years to come, maybe even get a Pulitzer for his flowery prose.

He allowed himself to fantasize as he sat at his desk in the spacious newsroom. He leaned back in his swivel chair, pushing away from the desk where his Remington typewriter rested and closed his eyes. Certainly, there were women in his future as he became famous. Maybe even the doll in the apartment where he found the hero. What was her name? Abrams, Mary Abrams. That was it. He would definitely give her a prominent role in his treatise. She would be grateful of course. It didn't really matter if she was a Jew. He could be expansive since she was beautiful. If that didn't work out, he would turn to the Graves woman. That is if her burns didn't mar her delicate features.

He picked up the phone and dialed the *Columbus Star*. He would need a history of Joe Chester. As he waited for an answer on the other end, he figuratively crossed his fingers that he would learn something juicy about the guy's past. Maybe a scandal that would make his series even more sensational, for it wouldn't just be one article, but a story that could stretch out for over a week, maybe even a month.

The Star was owned by the same conglomerate that had purchased the Chicago paper. That would make it easier to deal with them. Let their cub reporters do the leg work while Blake Evans got the byline and the glory. The contented man almost fell asleep waiting for an answer, he was so satisfied with himself.

Suddenly a melodic voice came on the line. "This is *The Columbus Star*. How may I help you?"

He wanted to say, come to Chicago baby, and let me see what's behind that voice. Instead, he lowered his own vocal to try to sound sexy and stated calmly, "This is Blake Evans, reporter for the *Chicago Sun Express*. I need a favor running down a lead."

"Let me connect you to an editor. Maybe he can help you," and the line went dead.

It had to be five minutes later when someone answered. Evans was just about to hang up, thinking he'd been disconnected by a dumb operator. "Dombrowski here. You say you're from the *Sun Express*?"

"That's right. I'm working on a big story here. Maybe you've heard about it, the fire where somebody tried to kill a woman?" Normally, a reporter wouldn't share that much information with a rival newspaper, but this was sort of on the same team, being owned by the same people. He was sure the other paper wouldn't try to steal his byline.

"Yeah, there was something on the wire, but since it wasn't local, I didn't pay too much attention to it." As a professional courtesy, he added, "How can we help?"

"There's this guy Joe Chester. He saved the woman, and maybe even the whole apartment building and its residents. Says he's from Columbus. I need all the background you can get me. Verify his age, find out where he lived growing up, his marital status, rap sheet if there is one. You get the idea."

The guy named Dombrowski was becoming irritated, "You want us to do all your leg work for you, is that it?"

"Naw, I didn't mean it that way. I just thought we could rub each other's backs so to speak. Whenever you need anything out of Chicago, I'm your man," Blake hoped that would smooth the guy's feathers. Maybe he had come on too strong.

"Yeah, I'll see what we can do. Give me a number to get back to you."

Blake hoped his sigh of relief didn't come across the wire. He read off the letters and digits printed on the phone before thanking the editor and placing the receiver on its cradle. Things were working out.

His next stop was at the hospital. He hoped he could get in to see the Graves woman. It was between visiting hours. At the nurse's station, he flashed his newspaper credentials two feet in front of the face of a frowning woman in a pale blue uniform and stated matter-of-factly, "I came to see Judy Graves."

"Visiting hours are from 2–5 pm, young man," she was about his age, so the comment was condescending in its tone.

He decided to stretch the truth, "I'm working with the Chicago police on her case. I really need to check some facts."

"She's sleeping. I won't wake her up, and neither will you. 2 pm is only an hour and a half off. I'm sure you can drink coffee for that long in our lounge, which is on the first floor by the way," she didn't wait for a reply before turning and walking away.

Bitch, he thought, as he reluctantly took her advice and caught the empty elevator to the first floor. At least it would give him a chance to go over his notes, and any background he had before confronting the patient.

There was very little information in his notebook about Judy Graves. She was 22 years of age, he knew that. Her father had come to visit her at the hospital, but Blake had no idea who he was. He'd heard that the two had words before he left her bedside. What was that all about? Obviously, he would have to do a lot of running around to piece this whole thing together, but he was up to the job. After all, it was going to make him famous and bring in bundles of cash.

17

Judy Graves was released from the hospital in September, only four days after being admitted to the burn unit of intensive care. She was not fully recovered, but she was deemed ambulatory after she assured her attending physician there was someone at her apartment who could clean her wounds and change bandages regularly. She lied about that, but she needed to get away. She was aware that people died in hospitals if they lingered too long.

Judy's father had visited regularly while she was bedridden. Sometimes, he just peered through her window without disturbing her. She knew he was there, but she didn't let on. Other days, he entered her private cubicle, which he had paid for. If she appeared to be sleeping, he didn't awaken her. He seemed content just to sit by her bedside, sometimes holding her hand.

She decided perhaps she'd been hasty in dismissing him from her life. Besides, she needed him now, maybe even more than when she was a child. She had the hospital administrators call Vince Arrizano when she was ready to move back into her apartment.

When the two, father and daughter, arrived at the Alliant Arms, the super informed them her apartment, which had sustained significant damage in the fire that nearly took her life, was not habitable yet. When learning she would be released, he had assigned her another apartment on the same floor as the one she had occupied earlier. He'd taken the liberty of moving what furniture had not been destroyed into the new place.

The superintendent, whose name was Tony Angelo, was the nephew of the owner, though he had to be at least in his 50s. He'd had a few dealings with the pretty tenant, but he'd seen her from time to time when collecting rent and attending to routine maintenance at her apartment. He would have liked to ask her out, but he was very shy, and of course too old for her. Tony was Italian and a romantic, and though he was born in the United States, he had a slight accent, gleaned from his years in the household of his parents, who had immigrated from the homeland in Sicily. Judy thought he was cute for an old guy.

As she slept in her hospital bed, she'd had a recurring dream of a man bending over her. It was hard to make out his features, but she was sure she could recognize him if, in fact, he did exist. She knew he was not the one who tried to kill her, for that monster wore a mask, and his eyes seemed blank—not at all like the man in her dream, whose eyes were wide and expressive.

Vince Arrizano knew about the guy who had saved his daughter from the burning apartment. He would be eternally grateful. There were two jobs on his immediate list of things to be accomplished. He was a list maker. Perhaps it was because his short-term memory was not good. He was always forgetting things. Anyway, the first thing was to profusely thank his daughter's savior. Secondly, he needed to find the person or persons responsible for putting Judy in the hospital. He would never give up on that.

After depositing his daughter on her couch, which had been one of the items to survive the fire, he wandered down the hall to where he'd been told Joe Chester was staying. He knocked on the door. He didn't know if his man would be there, since he might work, and it was only a little after noon. He was actually surprised when the door opened and a man he had never seen before stood before him.

"Yes? Can I help you?" Alex thought the stranger at the door had probably come to see Mary.

Vince shuffled his feet slightly and stated, "I came to see Joe Chester. Are you him?"

Alex answered, nervously, "What did you want to see him about?" He thought this man might represent a danger to him.

Vince Arrizano was not used to being questioned. He always dominated the conversation, except with his daughter. On the other hand, this might be his guy, and the last thing he wanted to do was antagonize him. "I'm Judy Graves' father," he finally stated. For one of the few times in his adult life, he was uncomfortable. Here he was in the presence of the individual who had saved his daughter from sure death. How could one repay that?

"Won't you come in, Mr. Graves?" Alex figured he'd just use the girl's last name, having no other options.

"It's Arrizano. My last name. My daughter changed hers a while back," he answered, as he stepped farther into the room and took the nearest seat, which was the sofa to the right of the entranceway.

"Oh. Is she married?" It was a natural assumption.

Vince became uncomfortable again, "No. She just changed it."

Alex noticed his visitor's discomfort and dropped that line of conversation, "How is your daughter doing?" He hadn't visited her because he didn't really know her, and he had problems of his own.

"She moved back into the building today. I just brought her. She's still bandaged up pretty tight, and I'll have to help her for a while, but she'll be all right."

"Did they catch the guy who tried to kill her?" Alex hadn't read one paper or watched the news on TV since he arrived back in town. It just hadn't occurred to him.

"Naw," Vince started to say he'd take care of that problem, but he stopped himself. It was something better kept to himself.

"That's too bad. Nobody has the right to do that to a human being," he was going to say that's what we're fighting in Guadalcanal to stop, when he caught himself.

Arrizano was talking again, "Look, kid, is there anything I can do for you? I'll be indebted to you for life. What about if I give you cash, maybe a couple thou?"

Alex didn't hesitate, "I don't want a handout. What I really need is a job. Do you know where I can get one?"

"Don't you have one?"

Alex stammered, "I'm between jobs right now."

"I'll give you one myself. What can you do?"

"Well, I'm good with my hands, maybe carpentry, or auto work." He added, "I'll do anything."

You don't really mean that, Vince thought to himself. What he said was, "Come to my office tomorrow. We'll find you something. In the meantime, here's some dough."

He handed Alex a 100-dollar bill, "Get yourself some casual clothes, maybe some slacks and a dress shirt, if you don't already have them."

Alex hesitated, pulling his hands back, "I can't take your money. Anyone would have done what I did. I was just there."

"You're wrong about that, kid. People just look out for themselves. You're special, and I want to pay you for it." With that, he stuffed the bill in Alex's shirt pocket.

"What can I say?"

"Hey, you earned it, and then some." Then, Vince got another thought, "Look, I can't always be here when my kid needs me, to change bandages and stuff. Could you do that for me? I'll put you on the payroll right now. Just keep yourself available. How about it?"

Alex thought for a few seconds before answering, "I can do that. If you don't have another job for me right away, I'll be here," and he added, "I think."

"So you're hired. Here's two more C notes in advance." Once again, before Alex could object, he stuffed the bills where the other had gone.

When Judy's father had left, Alex reached into his pocket and pulled out the three 100-dollar bills. He'd had no idea what a C note was. He sat down, amazed at his apparent good fortune. The money would solve one of his problems. Just then, what did it matter if the others seemed insurmountable?

18

Alex wondered what Vince Arrizano did for a living. He certainly dressed well. His suit looked made of silk, and his wing-tipped shoes sparkled like those of the Marine Corps with their spit shine. How could anyone just peel off three 100-dollar bills from a large roll as his visitor did? It would take a lowly Marine years to accumulate such a bankroll, assuming all the bills were hundreds.

It was now time to start earning his money. It would be hours before Mary returned from her job. He walked down the hall past the burned-out apartment and knocked on Miss Graves' door.

"Who is it?" a weak, high pitched voice from inside responded.

It occurred to Alex at that point that she wouldn't know him. "My name is Joe Chester," he answered, using his new name. "I was hired by your father to help you."

"When was that?" she was very skeptical, which was reasonable, considering someone had tried to kill her.

"Just a few minutes ago." And he added, "I just live a few doors down from you."

Realizing she would be at the mercy of whoever opened the door, which was not locked, Judy Graves reached into her bedside drawer and extracted a .38 revolver her father had given her for just such a circumstance. He knew she wouldn't be able to get to the door to unlock it since she was still in discomfort and unable to move freely with her bandages.

"Come in, but I warn you I have a gun."

"That's not very encouraging," Alex was tempted to turn back the way he had come, but then he wouldn't be earning the money he desperately needed. He took a deep breath and opened the door.

He could see into her bedroom from where he stood, but the woman was out of sight. He assumed, correctly, she would be in bed, "I'm coming to where you can see me. Please don't shoot. I just got these clothes."

It struck her as funny, and she laughed, "How can you think of clothes when someone's pointing a gun in your direction?" Then she saw him and she chuckled some more. "I must admit you don't look dangerous," she said as she took in his appearance.

"Well heck ma'am, I could be a cowhand who just shoveled a load of manure." Actually, that's how he thought of his getup.

"What's your name, cowboy?" she asked as she lowered the pistol. "Oh right, you said Joe somebody."

"Chester's the last name. At your service."

"You look familiar. Have we met before?" and before he could answer, she continued, "Do you work for my father?" She hoped he would say no, since he was good looking, even with the crazy clothes.

"You were unconscious the first and last time I saw you, and yes I work for your dad, but only to help with your bandages."

Suddenly, she remembered—the face from her dreams, "You saved me, didn't you?" She moved slightly and cried out in sudden pain. The pistol dropped to the floor. She'd forgotten to release the safety anyway. It was just as well. The gun didn't fire as it bounced on the plush rug.

"Try not to move," Alex said as he stepped to the side of the bed and retrieved the gun from the floor. He then handed it back to her.

"Oh, that hurt. Your advice comes a little late," she winced again slightly as she lay back on her pillow.

"Did you get instructions on how often to change your dressing?"

"It's on the nightstand."

Alex reached over and picked up the paper with the notes. "It looks like you need to take a pain pill at least a half-hour before, and then I'm to change the bandages every day, after cleaning the burnt area with soapy water." He looked down at her. Her left arm was wrapped in white gauze, as well as what he could see of her upper torso. The sight of her caused him to ask, with a slight redness to his cheeks, "Will you be okay with that?"

Judy grinned mischievously, "I'll be fine. How will you be?"

19

Judy Graves was not a virgin, hadn't been for quite a while. But lying there in bed with the white sheets around her, and the bandages giving the feeling she was completely at the mercy of the world around her; one might have the impression she was pure and innocent.

She'd been only 14 and in Junior High School the first time she was with a boy. They were experimenting with the touches they'd heard about in the locker room and the playground. It was all right because they were going steady.

The two kids were supposed to be at a movie, but they had snuck into an abandoned house. There was no electricity in the spacious downstairs of the three-story building that—with its cobwebs and darkness—gave the impression of being haunted.

There were bedrooms upstairs, but they never made it that far. They fell on an old round carpet as dust rose and settled on their bodies. The coupling was painful for Judy and she let out a small scream. The aroused boy was not deterred, and he pressed even harder on the supple body beneath him. It was over in minutes. She was left with the feeling she'd been violated somehow, while he smiled at his conquest.

Judy never talked about the encounter, nor was there another. Her family moved shortly afterward, which was a good thing because there was talk about how easy she had been. Other boys were trying to be with her, to no avail since, in her mind, she would never be caught in that situation again. She only hoped she wasn't pregnant. She wanted marriage and a home and little ones, but how could you love a child brought into the world from such violence?

She would be 21 before another man would get close to her. His name was Eddie Smythe. He was a man of the world, and a good-looking guy, with a full head of curly dark, nearly black hair. He even had a small mustache which was neatly trimmed. His five o'clock shadow made him look even more manly to her. He was only slightly taller than her five-foot-four, and she would have liked him to be a little bigger. He always wore a double-breasted gabardine suit with a tie when he came calling.

She knew he worked for her father, and that's how they met. At that time, she didn't know about the business they were in. By the time she found out, it was too late. She thought she was in love with the suave Eddie, and he assured her he was not involved with any of her old man's dirty enterprises. That was a lie, but she bought it at the time.

Eddie hadn't come around for some time before Judy met the man who had saved her. She was sure he'd found someone else. It hadn't been love. She knew that by then. So when she was once again alone, it wasn't as heartbreaking as it might be. She was ready to move on.

Now here was a man standing by her bed who was very attractive. She had no idea if he was available, but she would find out.

"Let me look at your arm," Alex said, interrupting her thoughts.

She held it out to him, wincing slightly, causing him to reply, "I don't want to hurt you, but it's probably time to change the dressing. Why don't you take one of your pain pills, and then I'll come back and do my work?"

"Where are you going?"

"I want to check on some things down the hall. How about I come back in about an hour? That should give your medicine time to work," he started for the door without waiting for her answer.

"I'll take the pill, but you don't have to leave," she liked his company, but she didn't say that. It didn't matter because he was already out of range of her weakened voice.

When he got back to Mary's apartment, she wasn't home yet. He didn't really have anything to do so, to kill time before he returned to Judy's place, he turned on the TV. A western movie was in progress. He recognized Richard Dix. Shoot-em-ups weren't really his thing, but he stretched out on the couch and watched anyway. Before long, his eyes drooped and he fell asleep.

He awoke about an hour and a half later and cursed himself for being late returning to the convalescent woman. He quickly washed his face to refresh himself and trotted down the hall.

Judy was still in bed, naturally. She admonished him for being late, "I thought you'd forgotten me, or maybe you didn't want to be bothered with my imperfect body." She tempered the harsh words with a smile, or rather, a grin.

"Right now, you're my life's work. Are you ready for the unveiling of your mummy's outfit?"

"I guess I'll just have to grin and bear it," she'd heard that phrase in a movie.

He found the end of the gauze and began slowly unwinding it. When her arm was clear, he took her hand, not wanting to touch where she'd been burned. He could see some dead skin and puffiness on her upper arm. Her wrist to her elbow seemed to be all right. He gently laid her arm back on the bed and went into the bathroom. There he found a washcloth and some liquid soap.

Walking back to her bedside, Alex told her, "I'm going to clean the wound, but I'll try to be gentle. Let me know if you feel any discomfort."

Judy got a worried look on her face and answered, "I'll try."

His touch was actually soothing in one respect since it was a man's touch, but she felt a strong stinging as he gently rubbed the dead skin from her arm, and cleaned the entire area with the soap. The hospital staff had given her a salve to use after cleaning. He patted the area dry, applied the ointment, and then rewound her arm with the fresh gauze, securing it with a clip that had been used before.

"Okay, we got through that. Now comes the hard part. I have to do the same for your stomach and above," he blushed as the implication became clear to them both.

She smiled, "Well if you must, you must."

He pulled the sheet down and left it at the foot of the bed. It seemed the end of the bandage that covered most of her upper body was near her navel. He found the clip, removed it, and placing his right hand on the back of Judy's neck, he lifted her slowly. She could feel a pinching of skin under the dressing, but she could handle it. She remained quiet, watching his face as he sat her up.

After he had removed some ten feet of gauze, he studied her completely uncovered upper body. Her breasts, which naturally caught his eye first, because he was a normal man, were firm and not sagging at all. Her nipples were pink, and more importantly, free of burns. That was not the case for her lower breasts. They were the same as with her arm. He would have to clean that part. The burns extended all the way down to just above her crotch, which was visible to him. Her back was the same.

As Alex cleaned her body as he had done her arm, there was a mixture of moderate stinging pain, and yet also pleasure, as he touched sensitive areas. Judy was amazed at how gentle he was. It was almost as if he was caressing her like a lover. She had never felt such tenderness. *This is a man I have to learn more about*, she thought to herself as she enjoyed his touch just below her now hard nipples.

If Alex O'Bannion was beginning to feel comfortable in his surroundings, there were two men who were about to change everything.

Sergeant Bill Helmand had just received his report from the Columbus police. He was puzzled. Chester had obviously lied to him about coming from the Ohio City. *Why?* He wondered.

They had clear prints from the Graves woman's apartment, and the results were not conclusive. Chester's would have been there from when he saved her, and the superintendent's seemed not to be important. The proper workings in the apartments were his responsibility. His prints would naturally be in all the rooms. Denton was another story. He'd have to follow up on that. The same with this guy Smythe. Maybe then the mystery would be cleared up...but he still liked Chester for it. Helmand decided to interrogate Chester again, but this time in the room specially designed for that type of discussion, at the station.

When he arrived at the Alliant Arms, he was disappointed to find no one home at the apartment of Mary Abrams. He should probably have gotten a search warrant to scour the residence. He made a mental note to do just that. A judge should grant the document since Chester had been elevated to number one on a very short suspect list.

As he passed down the hall, it occurred to Helmand he should touch base with the Graves woman. Maybe, now that she was lucid, she could shed some light on who attacked her and nearly killed her. Right now, in his mind, one Joe Chester was primed to go up for it, but his conviction could be overturned, should she provide an eyewitness identification of someone other than the mystery man Chester.

Just as he was about to knock on the lady's door, a deputy stepped out from the top of the stairs at the other end of the hall. "Hey Chief, I've been looking for you."

"Oh yeah, why?"

"We've got some more info on those prints from the FBI."

Blake Evans got the call he was waiting for as he sat at his desk in the copy room of the *Sun Express*. He'd been impatient for something to happen. He had a picture, albeit not a very good one, of Joe Chester. It was taken at the girl's apartment right after the fire. The guy was bare from the waist up, and his head was turned so that it would be hard for anyone to recognize him, but it was all he had. Evans was going to use it with his follow-up to his first piece about the mysterious hero. He hadn't yet learned who Judy Graves' father was. Had he known; the story might have taken a very different slant. The reporter, who was brilliant in his own mind, was concentrating so hard on building up Joe Chester, he was blind to events and people that might have really juiced up his soon to come follow-up article. He'd been sitting at his desk for over an hour and he had only a blank sheet of paper in his typewriter when the call came in. He didn't even have the headline yet.

"Hello," he answered, having not been told by the paper's receptionist who was on the other end of the call.

"Is this Blake Evans?"

"Yeah, who is this?" Evans had been deep in thought, and he resented the interruption, even though he'd been waiting for just that call.

"This is Eldon Dombrowski. You asked me for help finding a guy named Joe Chester here in Columbus, remember?" he too was showing impatience. After all, it was he who was doing the favor.

"Yeah. Sorry. I didn't recognize your voice, and I was working on something important. What did you find out?"

"Nothing. I mean the guy doesn't exist as far as being from here in Columbus. I checked the census and the police records. Nobody ever heard of him, and he's not on any paperwork anywhere. He's a phantom."

20

When Mary arrived home after work, Alex wasn't there. She worried that he might have left town. She didn't know about the arrangement with Vince Arrizano. She was sure he didn't have any money. Had he asked, she would have emptied her savings account for him, but of course, he didn't ask. While at work, she had checked to see if there were any openings there and was told nothing was available at the time.

Since she was obviously alone, she took the opportunity to take a bath. She had thrown her work clothes on the bed and was just stepping into the tepid water when she heard the front door open. She hadn't closed the door to her bathroom. She quickly jumped out of the tub and was about to close the door when Alex appeared before her.

"Wow," he exclaimed, in an appreciative tone, as Mary reached back for a towel to cover herself, turning a mild shade of red as she did so. She said nothing.

Alex reached through and closed the door between them, saying, "I'm sorry Mary. I had no idea I was interrupting your privacy."

While Mary was rationalizing the encounter in her mind, Alex was marveling at his luck in seeing two women at various stages of undress in the same day. He found himself comparing the two ladies he considered beautiful. Mary was a little shorter, and she seemed to have a narrower waist. Her freckles covered her whole body, but that was not a detriment in Alex's mind. Their breasts, which naturally caught the eye of the beholder first, were very similar and did nothing to detract from their beauty. Judy had a dark mole at the point of her right breast where it began to swell downward toward her nipple. All things considered, he thought Mary would win in a contest. His thoughts were interrupted as Mary—wrapped in a giant towel—came out of the bathroom.

"Do you mind leaving my bedroom so I can get dressed?" she was trying to be as matter of fact as possible to detract from what had just happened.

Now it was his turn to turn red, "I'm really sorry Mary." He wanted to add, "But you are beautiful." He restrained himself. The timing was not right.

"It was my fault. I could have closed the door," at the same time, she wondered why she hadn't done just that. Could it be she wanted him to walk in at that moment? She was definitely attracted to him. *Hussy!* she thought to herself, but then she smiled. She hoped his attributes didn't include mind-reading.

Apparently, they didn't, for he walked into the living room without a word. She was almost dressed when she heard pans rattle in the kitchen. When she came out of the bedroom, she saw he was assembling their dinner.

"I went to the store and bought some chow," he reverted to the military slang for food.

"How did you manage that? What did you use for money?" she said, as she sat on her couch watching him.

"I used money," he knew what she was getting at, but he decided to play with her.

"And where pray tell did you get it?"

"I had a visitor while you were gone. He offered me 300 dollars to change the bandages of his daughter, Judy Graves." He added, "He paid me in advance."

Mary screwed up her face in a curious look, "Just where are these bandages?"

"Oh, on her arm, and other places," Alex was strangely enjoying the banter between them.

Mary felt no such enjoyment. *Could it be*, she thought, *that I'm jealous*? She said out loud, "I thought I smelled something antiseptic about you."

Alex laughed. It was good to laugh. He actually forgot his predicament for the moment, "I had to rub a cream on the burns after I cleaned them."

She was jealous! "Was she beautiful?" She really wanted to say, "Am I as pretty as her?"

"She was okay. But she doesn't hold a candle to you," he lied.

"That was a nice thing for you to say. Now fix our dinner. What did you get?"

"Spam and beans," he kidded. "No, actually I bought a rump roast and potatoes You already have string beans. It's going to take a little while. Why don't you put some music on while we wait?"

"That sounds delicious. What are you going to do with the potatoes?"

"I thought I'd bake them with the roast. Is that okay?"

"Perfect," Mary answered, as she moved to the phonograph. "Do you like the Mills Brothers?"

"Not enough to go out with them, or fix them dinner, but their music is good."

As the sounds of *Till Then* drifted out over the room, Alex walked over to Mary and said, "May I have this dance?"

She answered by holding out her arms to him. He moved to her and put his hands on her shoulders. She tried to move closer, but he stopped her. "Don't get to close to me, Mary Abrams. You'll get hurt."

She didn't understand, "What do you mean?"

"I'm only half a man. You don't want to buy into that."

"I'm a grown woman. I make my own decisions," she tried once again to move closer.

He resisted, keeping her at arm's length. "The Marines would put me away if they could find me. I have no future, and I can't find my past."

She pushed toward him, and this time he let her in. "We can find your family together," she whispered, as her feet moved slowly to the music, and she placed her cheek against his shoulder. "Besides, you've seen me in the altogether. That means I'm yours forever," she held her breath to await his answer. It wasn't what she had hoped for.

"I'm married."

"What?" she replied disbelievingly, as she moved back.

"I wanted to tell you before, but for some reason, I couldn't."

She walked to her couch and sat down, "Where is your wife? Is she here in town?"

"I don't know. It was 1942 the last time I saw her. We weren't getting along. She might have gotten a divorce. I have to find her to learn where we stand. I don't love her anymore if that makes any difference." He paused to catch his breath, "I would have still given the marriage a chance, until I met you, if that matters."

"It doesn't. I don't know what you think of me, but I'm no home breaker," she began to weep softly.

He started for her, but she held out her arm with her palm out and said, "Don't."

His shoulders slumped perceptibly, and he turned toward the entranceway.

She looked up, saying, "Where are you going?"

"I've got to resolve this thing. I'll be back later," and he was out the door. Dinner never made it to the oven.

21

When the knock interrupted him, he was deep in thought. Tony Angelo had a hard time coming to grips with what had been happening at his apartment building. The Alliant Arms was a clean decent place. The four-story complex located only three miles from the heart of downtown Chicago had never had a hint of scandal since it was erected in the 1930s. Now, in the space of four years, there'd been two incidents.

The super was mulling over this latest episode, while sitting at his kitchen table, and looking out the window toward the busy part of town, with its skyscrapers shielding the lower part of the sky, which on that day was blue.

Tony was an easygoing third-generation Italian, who tried to avoid trouble. He was accommodating to a fault, not wanting to ruffle the feathers of any of his tenants, whom he considered his children. Some people had kids, others dogs, or cats, or both. With Tony, it was the people he served. When he got a call that something was wrong with one of the dwellings inside his building, he immediately reacted and took care of the problem. Most of the time, he could fix whatever it was that had busted or sprung a leak. If it was beyond his expertise, which seldom happened, he called an expert in.

Tony was getting up in years though, pushing 60, and he wasn't as spry as when he was younger. Still, he trudged up the stairs whenever he was called. The balding, paunchy five-foot-eight man was sustained by being needed. He had no living relatives, had never been married, and would have been extremely lonely were it not for his tenants. He hesitated to let them go when they sought him out, for he craved conversation and companionship.

When he answered the knocking, he was surprised to see the man he knew as Joe Chester standing there outside his door. Tony had only seen him once, when he raced upstairs on the day of the fire. He arrived on the second floor just in time to see a man dressed only in his underwear, carrying a limp woman in his arms toward an opening at the next-door apartment. His back had been turned, and Tony didn't get a look at his face then, but he had a clear view a minute later, as he stood frozen, still by the stairs, and watched the same individual rush into the room, which was filled with smoke. He was carrying a fire extinguisher. Tony finally reacted, running back downstairs to his apartment, where he called an operator and recited the address for the fire department.

Not five minutes later, the firemen arrived at the scene and quickly had the situation under control. Tony had followed the uniformed men upstairs. When he reached the adjacent apartment, he saw firemen calmly attaching an oxygen tank to the woman who appeared to be burned. The unclothed fellow was standing back, watching. Tony had the strange feeling he knew the man, or at least that he had seen him before.

Now, at the door to his own apartment, he had the same impression. Then it came to him. This guy was a dead ringer for the man who had been killed there in 1948. Only that time, there was a large, bloody butcher knife sticking out of the victim's throat.

"I'm sorry to bother you," Alex began, "but I was told you are the superintendent of the building."

"That's right, Mister Chester. What can I do for you?" Tony was feeling a little nervous, considering.

"I'm looking for someone, and I hope you can help me. They used to live here. They moved in about when the war began."

"Which war? I came in 1945. Were they here then?"

"Yes. I think we, I mean they, moved in around 1941," Alex hoped the super didn't catch his slip.

"What were their names?" Tony could have told him who they were at that point. The memory of the murder was vivid in his mind.

"Jack O'Bannion and his wife and daughter. I lost touch with them sometime in the forties, and I'd really like to find them. Can you help?" Alex had a hopeful look for the first time in a while, "Were you here then?"

"What's your relationship with these people?"

Alex didn't answer immediately. He was supposed to be a cousin of Mary Abrams. Finally, he did say, "They were just friends of the family. As I remember, they were great people."

"I did know them," Tony answered. Alex heaved a sigh of relief. Maybe his search was ending.

"Do you know where they are?"

Tony Angelo was really confused. None of this made any sense to him. Here stood a man who Tony himself had seen lying on a blood-soaked bed with a knife in his throat, and he was asking about people who were also deceased. Sweat began dripping from his forehead as he yelled, "Get away from me! You're dead!" as he pushed a bewildered Alex back from the doorway and slammed the door.

22

The mystery of the fire and attempted murder at the Alliant Arms apartments was about to take a dramatic turn, and it would be Alex O'Bannion who ironically would provide the clue that would eventually break the case.

It began innocently enough. Police Sergeant Bill Helmand put out a bulletin for all beat cops to be on the lookout for one Joe Chester, who was a suspect in the case. He had contacted the newspaper to retrieve the one photo of the suspect, and that was attached to the circular. Helmand really was interested in why his suspect had lied to him about coming from Columbus.

It didn't take long to locate Chester. As it happened, he was on his way to the library after his encounter with Tony Angelo. He was in a slight daze as he rode on the El, the elevated train. He had no idea what set the super off like that. Was he a raving lunatic? Or was there a key to decipher what the man had said? He was still pondering what had happened when he stepped off the train downtown after his short ride. He felt the central library would provide a better chance to find information. He wanted to check the latest published census for the city to see if any members of the O'Bannion family were listed, and peruse old newspaper clippings on the off chance there had been a story about any of them. He was walking innocently down the block leading to his destination when a policeman walked up to him. Alex had no reason to lie when the cop asked him if he was Joe Chester, since that was the name he was going by, and he was not in any trouble as far as he knew. He was nervous for another reason. Should anyone learn of his true identity, it could mean a death sentence, were he not able to explain his disappearance from the battlefield…a fact he himself didn't understand.

The beat cop followed protocol and asked for identification. When his suspect was naturally unable to produce it, the uniformed policeman placed Alex under arrest, handcuffing him. He walked his prisoner to a phone on a nearby corner and called for a cruiser to transport him to the stationhouse.

Alex was placed in an interrogation room once he and his police escort arrived at police headquarters. It was only a matter of minutes before Detective Sergeant Helmand entered the room and took a seat across a wide table from him.

"You're a hard man to track down, Chester," he began.

Alex shuffled his feet nervously, feeling this could not turn out well for him, "I didn't know you wanted to see me, or I would have come in on my own."

"I'll get right to it. Why don't you have any identification?"

Alex thought quickly. Maybe he could delay the inevitable, "It's in my other pants back at Mary's apartment. I just forgot it when I changed."

"We'll check on that."

"Why was I picked up?"

"Well, I'll tell you, son," he began, in a condescending tone, "You are a suspect in the apartment fire, and I have a few questions for you."

"Are you officially charging me?"

"We may, depending on your answers here." Actually, they had nothing to charge him with at that point, but they were hoping he would slip up under questioning. Had Helmand known who he really was, the questions would have been quite different.

"I want to help, but I'm not sure I know anything more than you already know. I didn't see anyone else when I went into the girl's room, and the hall was clear when I came out. No, wait a minute. There was a man, I think it was a man, standing by the stairs at the end of the hall. I didn't think anything of it at the time."

"Yeah, that might have been the super of the building. He told us he saw you carrying the woman back to the Abrams place. Did you know Judy Graves before you rescued her?"

"No. I just smelled the smoke, as I told you before."

Alex wondered where this line of questioning was headed.

"Funny, the same super saw you leaving her room earlier today!"

"I can explain that. Her father hired me to keep an eye on her, and to change her bandages every day. He felt Judy would trust me since I saved her."

"Oh yeah, her father. He came to the hospital to see her too. It's funny, though; we talked to the woman, and she said her father was dead. So who is this mystery guy?"

"He introduced himself to me as Vince Arrizano."

"What! Vince Arrizano is Cosa Nostra. He's the crime boss of South Chicago. Hell, he might even run the whole city as far as I know." He paused, with a look of consternation on his face, "You're telling me Arrizano is Judy Graves' father?"

Alex was just as shocked as Helmand, "That's what he told me."

"Stay put. I'll be right back." With that, his interrogator got up and went out the door, leaving Alex to wonder what was going on. What the hell had he gotten himself into?

Helmand went directly to his chief's office. "There's been a new wrinkle in the Graves case, Chief. It turns out the crime boss of the south side could be her father."

"Wait a minute. I've got something about that on my desk," he rifled through some stacked papers and pulled one out. "It says here the murdered guy they found in Indiana was a hood named Ed Smythe. He was working for Vince Arrizano. He was a hired gun."

Helmand was shocked, "I never got this info. How come?"

The chief brushed that off, "I just received it today from the FBI. They were working the case because Smythe had an Illinois address, but he was found in Indiana. That's crossing state lines."

"I'll be damned!"

"Didn't you run a check on the girl's history?" the chief asked the obvious question.

"She was a victim. I should have followed up on that end, but I hadn't gotten around to it yet."

"I suggest you do. Meanwhile, cut the Chester guy loose. We can always pick him up later."

Helmand did exactly that when he came back to the interrogation, "You're free to go, Chester. Stay close."

After Alex was gone, Helmand remembered the reason he had the man hauled in in the first place. His brain had completely short-circuited when he learned who Judy Graves' father was. He still didn't know why Joe Chester, if that really was his name, had lied about coming from Columbus. That didn't seem important at that moment, but an abstract thought crossed the mind of the policeman. What if Joe Chester was really a criminal or a key witness in a federal case in some other state, and he was in the witness protection program of the United States Government? He could even be a murderer. With that past, he could have been hired to do the hit on Judy Graves, and Ed Smythe too. But that still left the question of who hired him. Vince Arrizano was looking good for that, but would he kill his own daughter?

Alex felt he had dodged a bullet as he left the police station. It was only a matter of time until the authorities learned he had no identification showing he was Joe Chester because he wasn't. He was Alex O'Bannion, deserter, and God knows what else. There was still the matter of the missing ten years.

It was too late to visit the library, and he was an unwelcome guest at Mary's place. That left only one option in his mind. He headed to the local YMCA. At least he had enough money for the night's lodging.

23

It should have been so simple. Why do things always have to turn out so complicated? It started out to be a good plan. I learned from one of her coworkers in a casual conversation that she always had Thursday afternoons off. She could have had other intentions and not even gone home, but my luck was holding so far. No one saw me as I went up the stairs after I saw her. She did glance my way down the hall as I stood there, but she didn't react since she didn't know me. It was afternoon, and all the other tenants should have been at work.

No one was in the hall on her floor as I casually opened her unlocked door. Up until then, everything was working like clockwork. The hood was probably a good idea, as were the gloves. She was either in her bedroom or bathroom as I donned my disguise. I only used them in case something went wrong. As it turned out, it was good that I did, seeing as how she was still alive and could identify me. It was as if I was never there, except for one thing. I had intended to kill her, set the place on fire, and then get the hell out of there. But when I saw her there, she looked too beautiful to pass up. She was easy to overpower. She passed out or fainted, I don't know which. After I had my way with her, and she hadn't woken up, I just set the place on fire. Then I went to my room on the first floor, thinking the flames would rise, and I would be safe down below.

I heard the commotion as the firemen and police arrived on the scene, but I didn't learn the rest of it until I read it in the paper the next day.

So here we are. She's still up there in her apartment, with only some burns to show for it. But I'm not done with her. My time will come again. She can't just get up and go on with life, not with the burns that should have killed her. If any guy gets close to her, I'll kill him too.

24

Blake Evans was confused. As he sat at his small desk in the expansive copy room of the *Sun Express*, he wondered why the man he knew as Joe Chester had lied to him. Blake was too new at the game of reporting to sense when someone wasn't telling the truth...too new at life for that matter.

The sinewy, athletic-looking man-boy was but 22 when he came to work at the paper...not old enough to have sampled life or its inhabitants. In school, he would have been labeled a nerd, were it not for his inherited athletic ability. He excelled at just about any sport. He had been put in school at a younger age than the other kids in his class. It was a recommendation from his family doctor. Blake was a nervous kid, always needing to be on the go. His mother was afraid he'd get in trouble without any activity, so she lied about his age, putting him in kindergarten at the age of four. She had good intentions, but he soon developed an inferior complex, trying to compete with older, bigger kids. Sure he was good enough to play, just not as strong or talented as the boys who made first string. He would dutifully sit on the bench, waiting his turn to show what he could do, but it was usually in the last seconds of the basketball game when the contest was out of reach one way or the other. In football, it was the same. One thing that did come out of it though was the molding of his body. As a sophomore in high school, he weighed a less than imposing 126 pounds, but with the conditioning drills and weightlifting required of the sports, he was close to 200 pounds by the time he reached his senior year. He had no trouble making first string that year, and he led his team to the league championship. He was 17. By the time he reached college, his body weight had reached 220. At Notre Dame, he soon became the backup fullback.

In school, he'd taken journalism as his English class in his senior year. He fell in love with it. The political story he had stumbled on got his foot in the door at the *Sun Express*, and he was determined to make it his life's work.

Now here he was, with possibly the story of a lifetime almost handed to him, and he had been thrown a curve that threatened to sabotage all his dreams, or at least delay them.

Why had Chester lied? What did he have to gain by it? He must have known he would be found out, if not by him, then by the police.

Blake sat there, a copy of the photo on his desk, along with the outline of the story he'd already begun. It would have to be completely reworked. He would have to start back at the beginning, when he had walked into Mary Abrams' bedroom and seen Joe Chester naked from the waist up on the other side of the bed. A thought occurred to him. Were they lovers? All he had to go on about them being cousins was Chester's word. Hell, that might not even be his real name. How could he have been so easy? He scribbled words on the scratchpad in front of him. Name was one, with Alias under it. Marital Status was the next. Underneath, he wrote Check Census. The third item, since the Korean War had not been completely resolved, was Military Service. He realized if he didn't learn the real name of his quarry, the rest would be an exercise in futility.

Who was Mary Abrams? He had taken her at face value too. She worked as a clerk at Woolworth's was what she'd said. Even that could be a lie. Where did she come from, and how long has she known Joe Chester? Maybe she'll know his real name.

Okay. Now we're cooking. How about Judy Graves? Where does she fit into this puzzle? Is she really a victim? Where did she come from? Who are her parents? Did she know her attempted killer—or Joe Chester, for that matter?

The blonde, well-tanned reporter was becoming excited. He wasn't dead in the water yet. No sir. He would show them all. This would become an exposé, forget the tear-jerker about the all-American hero.

He practically ran to the door to run down his first lead, Mary Abrams. The way he saw it, the only way he could find out Joe Chester's real name was from the woman who was possibly his girlfriend. Failing that, his next step would be to grill Judy Graves.

Mary stretched out on her bed, even though it was too early for sleep. She hadn't even fixed dinner. The thought hadn't occurred to her. She had other things on her mind. Would Alex come back? Even though she'd been upset, there was still something between them. She couldn't deny that. She was even a little jealous of the bedridden woman down the hall, as silly as that was.

When she heard the knock on the door, she jumped up, happy Alex had changed his mind and returned to her. She flung the door open and a shocked look appeared on her face as she realized it wasn't Alex. "What are you doing here?" was all she could think of to say, as she looked at the reporter Blake Evans standing there.

25

Except for a stiff back from sleeping on a thin mattress, Alex was reasonably refreshed when he awoke that Friday morning at the Young Men's Christian Association in downtown Chicago. He'd gotten a good night's sleep in spite of the perceived insurmountable problems ready to overwhelm him with the light of day.

There was only one item on his agenda for the morning, the library. After that, it would depend on what, if anything, he learned there. He was still walking around in the jeans, shirt, and shoes Mary had bought him, so add shopping to the list.

Thinking of Mary made him sad. Perhaps in another place and time, they would have had a future together. At least it would have been worth pursuing. She was a sweet kid who didn't deserve what he had put her through.

The library was right where Mary had told him. It was a huge building with many large windows. The architecture was like something Frank Lloyd Wright might have designed. He had to walk up a flight of stairs to the entrance. He noticed the gardening around the front of the structure was immaculate, with short clipped very green grass and hedges framing the landscape, and separating it from the sidewalk. Alex wondered how the city could afford such a magnificent showpiece.

He walked in, found the information desk, and asked the older woman with spectacles hanging from the end of her nose where he might find a copy of the Illinois census. She replied, curtly, that one would have to go to the city office to find that. After thanking her, Alex asked where he could locate old newspapers. She brightened at that. She could indeed help him there. She pointed to her right, "You'll find those down that last aisle, young man." She was looking at his clothes, with a disapproving look on her face as she spoke. Alex thanked the woman and headed in the direction she had pointed.

Against an outside wall, there was a huge rack that was stuffed with old copies of the *Chicago Sun Express*. The papers were organized with the newest copies at the bottom. Alex reached out to a middle shelf and pulled one paper out. The date was September 1st, 1947. He assumed the ones behind the paper he had were later dates of the same month and year. He was right.

Sitting at a large desk in front of the display, he spread out the sheets. It wasn't likely he would be lucky enough to find anything helpful in locating his family with the first paper, but he had to begin somewhere.

The sun was setting behind the tall buildings to the west when he finally exited the library, disappointed, but realizing he was looking for the proverbial needle in the haystack with the method he had chosen. His odds were worse than a thousand to one that he would be able to locate even one member of his family. Oh well, there was still the census.

It was too late to find the city office that day, he was sure. And he needed to get to Judy Graves' apartment to attend to her bandages. It was a little too far to walk, and he was tiring, so he found the El platform. At least this time, he had change.

It was rather funny when he had tried to cash one of his large bills at the changemaker booth earlier. The clerk had told him he was crazy. He wasn't a bank. Alex had to find a store to get change. Even then he was looked at strangely as he handed the checker his 100-dollar bill in payment for a five-cent candy bar. He got his change though.

As he was walking up the stairs to the second floor, Alex got an idea. The police would know if anything had happened to any member of his family. But he couldn't just walk in and ask. He was known to law enforcement as a suspect in an attempted murder case. What if he got someone else to check for him? It would have to be a person he could trust to tell the truth. Up till now, there was only one individual who was in that category, Mary Abrams. He was persona non gratis to her right now, so it had to be someone else, but who? One other name came to mind, Vince Arrizano. If he was such a bad guy as Helmand had claimed, then he wouldn't blink at the quandary of Alex O'Bannion. It was worth a shot.

When he reached Judy's door, he nodded to the patrolman sitting in a wooden chair outside her apartment. "How's she doing today, officer?" he greeted.

"I think she's awake. Did you come to change her bandages?"

"Yep. Has her father been here today?"

"I just came on at 4 pm. I'm not sure."

"Thanks anyway," Alex answered as he walked into Judy's living room.

The patrolman had been alerted to Alex's status, but he was just told to keep an eye out for anything suspicious. He'd been the same one who had admitted Alex the day before, and nothing untoward had occurred then, so he wasn't too worried. He would, however, open the door in a few minutes to make sure everything was okay. He might even get a peek at the woman in a state of undress.

Judy was sitting up with her pillow supporting her back against the headboard when Alex walked in. "Hi, Judy. How goes it?" he greeted her.

"I missed you," she replied

"That's not what I meant. How do you feel?"

"A little better, I guess. I'm getting stiff just lying here though."

"We could go dancing," he joked.

Her face took on a sad look, with the corners of her mouth drooping, "I'm not in the mood for banter. Tell me how pretty I look in this outfit." She pointed toward the loose-fitting shirt that covered her wrapped torso.

"You know you're cute. I don't have to tell you that."

Then he changed the subject, "Has your dad been in today to check on you?"

"No. Do you know about him?"

Alex played dumb, "No. What do you mean?"

"What he does for a living."

"You tell me," he was curious about how she would respond.

"He's a gangster. He has people rubbed out. You know, killed," her eyes were wide, as she waited for his reaction.

"You've been seeing too many George Raft movies."

Just then, as if on cue, Vince Arrizano walked into the room, "Am I interrupting anything?"

Alex spoke first, "No. I was just about to change her bandages and clean the wounds. I'm glad you showed up though, I need to talk to you."

"Oh? What about?"

"Can you stick around for a while? Let me change Judy's bandages, then we can talk."

"Sure, kid. I'm a man of leisure today anyway."

With that, Judy turned her head away.

"I'll just wait in the other room. Take your time," Vince said as he walked out.

About a half-hour later, after Alex had completed his work, and Judy laid back down to take a nap, he went out to where the older man waited, closing the door to her bedroom.

"I need a favor, Mr. Arrizano," he began, "but I want to fill you in on something first. Maybe we can go to the coffee shop down the street and let Judy rest."

"Sure. We can do that."

When they were settled in a booth, Arrizano started with, "Call me Vince, kid. Shoot. I'll do what I can. I owe you big time."

"You may not feel that way when you hear what I have to say."

"What is it? Got too many parking tickets?"

"I wish that was it. I'm not who you think I am."

26

It was another clear crisp day. There'd been many in this election year along the Pacific Coast. From Gloria's perch on her deck high above the cliffs of La Jolla, California, she appreciated the break in the coastal clouds. It was one of the reasons they had made the decision to move, she and Carl. You could have your seasons. As she looked out over the broad expanse of water, perhaps as far as 30 miles, she compared the view to that of Lake Michigan. The lake was pretty and serene, on those days one could see it, or venture out into the sub-freezing weather. They had heard of the even climate along the coast of Southern California. It turned out to be a good trade.

None of it could have happened without Carl. As she sat there, wrapped in a blanket, alone on one of the two lounge chairs facing out to sea, she remembered how it was.

She was barely 18 when she met Carl Windsor. She was far too young to know what she wanted out of life. She'd just gone through the tragedy of losing both her parents, and she was living with her brother and his new wife in a crowded apartment on the south side of Chicago. She was still a senior in high school. Her surviving brother Alan would drop her off at school on his way to work each weekday morning. She couldn't afford a car, and no one was going to buy her one.

It was weird, living with Alan and her sister-in-law. She had been married to Gloria's older brother Alex, but he was killed in the war. It didn't take Emily long to latch onto Alan, who was Alex's twin and reminded her of him. They were never close, perhaps because Gloria felt Emily was a schemer and opportunist. She blamed none of it on her brother.

Carl Windsor was 22 years old and a senior at Chicago University when they met. He hadn't gotten a scholarship, but his family was rich, and they paid his tuition. He had been offered free rides at various prestigious universities, but Carl, even at such a young age, knew what he wanted, and for him, Chicago University and their Meteorology degree program was the only place to be. He wanted to study thunderstorms and tornadoes, so he became a science major.

They met at a science fair offered by the university. He was manning a booth for extra credit, and she had stopped by with a female friend because Gloria had always had a fascination with astronomy. At that point in her life, it only included the constellations and their names.

As they talked that day, Carl found it easy to converse with the attentive, pert high school senior. Her friend had drifted away, in search of interesting boys, leaving Gloria to flirt with the college man. He was emboldened by her interest, which he perceived to be only about the science; she had no idea his family was rich, and she was attracted only because he was a good-looking older man. He wrote his name and phone number on the back of a business card the university had furnished, telling her she could call him if she had any more questions, about the science or the college, of course.

She waited a reasonable time, two days, before calling him. They made a date to meet over dinner. He took her to a restaurant along the Lake Michigan shore she would never have been able to afford. He was very attentive and asked about her life while offering nothing about himself. He had brought flowers, which he presented to her when he picked her up in what she believed was his family car, a late-model Cadillac. She thought he was just trying to impress her, not realizing that was his own car. All the boys she had known up till then drove old jalopies.

The romance progressed rapidly after that. It was only five dates over a span of two months before he dropped to his knees and proposed to her. They had shared only one kiss for each meeting, as he left her at her door wanting more.

The night he asked her to marry him was different. They went back to the same restaurant as their first date, but this time they were seated with a spectacular view of the lake. She had told him earlier when they discussed their taste in music that she loved *Moonlight Serenade* by the Glenn Miller orchestra. Suddenly the band, which usually played soft dinner music, went into the same arrangement as the recording. Gloria was about to remark how coincidental that was when she noticed her dinner date was kneeling at her feet. Suddenly she got it.

After she had accepted his proposal, she felt obligated to tell him that there was no way her family could pay for the wedding, and would he mind if they were married by a

Justice of the Peace? Her humility and willingness to sacrifice overwhelmed him. "There's no way I would have you miss a traditional wedding. I'm sure my family will foot the bill."

She wanted to object, but when she looked into his eyes and realized how resolute he was, she just answered, "I love you!"

She finally realized how rich his family was as she looked around the giant cathedral that was the setting for their union. The reception was held in the garden of the Abraham Lincoln Presidential Library in Springfield, Illinois. All the guests were transported there by separate limousines.

When he graduated, Carl wanted to be offered a position with the University in their Severe Storms laboratory, but he was disappointed to learn he would at least need a master's degree. Since he now had a wife, with a baby on the way, he took a position with the Scripps Institute of Oceanography in San Diego, California. His disappointment was tempered with the knowledge he wouldn't have to put up with violent winters any longer. The climate in San Diego was reputed to be the most even in the world.

The young couple was devastated when they lost the baby shortly after their move out west. Had they not been deeply in love, the marriage might not have survived. It would be two more years before the still young housewife was again with a child. She was ordered to bed in her third trimester, so as to not take any chances with this pregnancy. Her perfectly formed boy, at seven pounds even, was born late in 1951. They named him Carl Jr.

27

Oliver West and his entourage landed in Honolulu during a hurricane. The eye of the storm was actually 200 miles to the north, but it was raining heavily, with about 35 mile-an-hour winds. The passengers from the Pan Am flight were all drenched by the time they raced across the tarmac to the terminal. Oliver headed for the bar, while the others in the party waited for their baggage to be off-loaded. He felt he needed to unwind. One member of his group, who had unfortunately been sitting next to him on the window side of the plane, just wouldn't stop talking, preventing him from getting any sleep. It would have been all right had the woman been interesting, but all she could talk about was her husband's new business, and how they were going to be rich. Oliver occasionally nodded, or said, "That's nice," to be polite, but that just encouraged her to keep talking. When the plane landed, he couldn't get away from her fast enough.

In the lounge, while sipping on a Mai Tai, he finally relaxed enough to be able to look ahead. They had allocated three days to each island, which meant they wouldn't reach Guadalcanal for nearly three weeks. They'd planned stops at Oahu, Midway, and Guam before they hit the Solomons. They were going to fan out separately, and talk to as many of the soldiers, sailors, and Marines who had known one of the names on their list of missing as they could in the time allotted to them. They wanted eyewitness accounts of the event that led up to their buddies vanishing.

Oliver was on his second Mai Tai when he heard his name on the loudspeaker. He couldn't make out the message, but he assumed his bags were ready to be picked up. When he arrived at the baggage carousel, his were the only bags left. He was relieved that the others—including his chatty seatmate—had already gone their separate ways.

The cab that had chosen him dropped him off at his hotel downtown. He checked into his room, then immediately left again, after depositing his luggage there.

There were five names on his list. The one he decided to check on first was at Hickam Field. He would need to rent a car, so he once again hailed a cab to take him back to the airport. He cursed himself for not just getting the rental while he was there in the first place. Maybe those drinks had an effect on him. But he felt he was perfectly sober by the time he got behind the wheel of his full-size Chevy. He was a fairly large man, and he liked the space behind the wheel afforded by the bigger vehicles.

The man he wanted to talk to was still in the service and stationed there at Hickam. Oliver found him at the motor pool. His name was Arnie Statham, and he was a Tech Sergeant with the now U.S. Air Force. It was just the Army Air Corps at the time his co-worker disappeared. It turned out the missing man wasn't missing at all. His head had been blown off, along with his dog tags when the Japs strafed the flight line on December 7th, 1941. Positive identification was impossible, so he was listed as missing in action. It was just a technicality. Everyone knew at the time who he had been. Oliver made a notation by the man's name, thanked his informant, and made his way back to Pearl Harbor.

By the time they left the Hawaiian Islands, they had only identified three men who would now be listed as deceased through their efforts, but the group had new hope as their journey continued because they had found one sailor actually alive. He'd been on the battleship Nevada and he was blown off the deck into the oily water in the harbor. He managed to make it to shore, but he had a concussion from the blast and no memory of who he was. His work uniform had been ripped from his body, and he didn't even know he was in the navy. He was found on the shore by a civilian family, who took him home to recover. When he finally remembered what had happened, it was 1942. He'd gone to work in town as a bartender, and he decided to remain there. Actually, he was a deserter, but after finally turning himself in after being tracked down by the group Oliver West belonged to, the navy declined to press charges, since it was ten years later. But he was no longer listed as missing and presumed dead.

When Oliver boarded the plane for the long trip to Guam via Midway, he was glad he had the window seat this time and the other seat was occupied by a man, who had no desire to divulge his life story.

28

Mary had a strong inclination to refuse the reporter admittance to her apartment, fearing she might let something slip. Then she remembered Alex had betrayed her by failing to mention he had a wife. For just an instant, she wanted revenge. *How could I let him get to me like this?* she thought. *I didn't even know him a month ago. Am I so insecure I'll let a stranger get that close?* Still, her protective instincts were in place, and she knew she wouldn't say anything to jeopardize her Marine, even though he was a heel.

"Won't you come in?" she cordially invited.

When Blake entered, he said, "I'm sorry if I disturbed you, but something's come up that I need your help with, to verify some information that's come into my possession." He waited for her to offer him a seat. She didn't.

"What is it?" she replied, irritably.

He realized that, by her tone, if this were a courtroom, Mary Abrams would definitely be a hostile witness. He would proceed accordingly.

"Why would your cousin lie about where he lived? We both know he didn't come from Columbus." So the battle lines were drawn. He took a step closer to her as a sign of intimidation.

She didn't flinch, holding her ground. Now she was getting mad. How dare this weasel come into her home and confront her like she was some criminal?

Evans could see she was stiffening up. She wasn't likely to give him what he wanted, as long as she saw him as an adversary. He smiled, "Look, Mary," using her first name might help, "I think we got off on the wrong foot here. I want to write a flattering article about Joe. I still feel he's a hero, but I don't think the police have that opinion. They're sure to find out he lied about his home, and they'll wonder why. If we can get the jump on them with this article, maybe they'll give Joe a break, and think he was just confused. Where did he come from?"

Was he telling the truth? Mary wondered. Could she really trust him? She decided to play dumb, "I don't know."

"Then he's not your cousin after all?" Evans was pleased that his friendly ploy worked. "Were you just protecting him when you said that?"

"Yes. I suppose so," she wished at that moment Alex was there to help her. She didn't want to get him in more trouble, but that's where the conversation was headed.

"Did you even know him before the day of the fire?" *Now we're getting someplace*, he thought to himself.

What could she say? She didn't want to perjure herself. She wasn't a liar. Alex had forced her to become one. She couldn't protect him anymore, "No." As she said the one word that betrayed him, she thought of the old uniform that she had hung carefully in her closet, after removing it from the bag Alex had stored it in. Perhaps it was dumb, but she didn't want it to get wrinkled. At least that was one secret she would hold onto, for she didn't understand it herself. "Now will you please leave my apartment? I'm very tired," her shoulders slumped, as if in testament to her words.

Blake Evans needed more, but he felt he'd reached a place of an impasse. She wasn't likely to reveal any new facts at that time. He thanked her for being candid and left.

Perhaps Judy Graves can fill in the blanks, in what is turning out to be a humdinger of a story, Evans thought, as he walked down the hall to the invalid's rooms. "That's strange," he said aloud, as he noticed the policeman assigned to protect the woman wasn't in the hallway outside her door. He knocked, not really expecting her to come and let him in. He just thought she might yell to let himself in. Instead, there was no sound coming from inside. He tried the door. It was locked. He knew for a fact the door had been left unlocked because she couldn't get out of bed to let anyone in.

At that moment, the man he knew as Joe Chester appeared down the hall at the top of the stairs.

Alex had just come from his meeting with Vince Arrizano at the coffee shop down the street. While there, he had told the mobster everything. He was at the point that he felt he had nothing to lose, and because of who Arrizano was, and what he felt he owed Alex, there was an excellent chance it wouldn't go any further.

After hearing Alex's version of the events leading up to his appearance at the door of Mary Abrams, the father of Judy Graves was just as confused as the man who sat across from him. He thought maybe Alex, for he now knew his real name, had amnesia from being wounded. He couldn't explain his still being in uniform, so he chose to ignore it for the moment. "So what do you need from me?"

"It would help if I had some identification proving I'm Joe Chester," and he added, "at least until I can explain things."

"I might just know someone who could arrange that."

"I was hoping you did," Alex was beginning to feel like maybe things would work out, and because of it, his thoughts returned to Mary Abrams. He couldn't blame her for how she'd reacted. He would have done the same under similar circumstances. He had to find Emily and straighten out his life. Then he would at least know how part of his life might turn out.

As he was leaving the coffee shop, after arranging to meet Arrizano the next day to pick up the credentials he'd been assured would be ready by then, he decided to try to explain things better to Mary. She should be home from work by then. He glanced down at his wrist, where his watch should be, and it wasn't there. He remembered removing it before he worked on Judy's burns. It must still be on her nightstand. The watch had been given to him by his father on the occasion of his acceptance to college. He had worn the watch in battle, even when he was advised against it. It was a piece of home he wasn't willing to give up.

As he reached the top of the stairs, Alex noticed Blake Evans with his hand on the doorknob of Judy Graves' apartment. "What are you doing here?" he yelled down the hall. Then he noticed the police guard was missing. "What the hell?" he muttered, suddenly breaking into a run toward Evans.

"The door's locked," the reporter told him. "That's not right, is it?"

Alex ignored the question, "Where's the cop? Did you send him away?" He thought maybe Blake had told the uniformed man he would watch out for whatever while the guy relieved himself, or got coffee.

"He was gone when I got here."

Suddenly the gravity of the situation struck Alex. He slammed his shoulder into the door. It didn't budge. Blake and Alex pushed at the same time, and the door finally gave way, splintering at the hardware holding it.

Alex was first stumbling into the room. He looked up, and there stood a man in a police uniform that he didn't recognize. He was near the door leading into Judy's bedroom, and he had a gun. It was pointed in Alex's direction.

Before Alex could react, there was an explosion. Then his reflexes took over. Before the gunman could fire again, Alex tackled him. The gun went flying as the man hit the wall behind him. Alex hit him with his closed left fist, his elbow following and colliding with the jaw of the intruder. The force of the second blow was strong enough to render the man unconscious. Alex retrieved the revolver, which was a .38. Then he heard a moaning behind him.

Blake Evans was bleeding from the neck. It appeared he was still alive. Alex quickly went to the bathroom of the apartment and got a towel. While keeping an eye on the still unconscious man near Judy's bedroom door, he pushed the towel against the wound on the reporter's neck.

A crowd was beginning to appear at Judy's front door. "Did someone call the police?" he yelled. "We'll need a medic too. This man's badly hurt."

A voice from in the hall called back loudly, "I called them, but I don't know about an ambulance."

"Will someone take care of that?" Alex responded.

Just then, two uniformed policemen showed up. Alex rose and rushed into Judy's bedroom. She lay there crying. Apparently, she was uninjured.

29

"What happened, Judy?" Alex asked the visibly shaken woman lying on the bed. "Are you all right?"

"I am now, thanks to you. That's the second time you've saved my life. That goon was just about to shoot me when you busted through the door. He heard the noise and went to see what happened."

"Who is he? Do you know him?"

"I never saw him before in my life," then she corrected herself, "except when he tried to kill me before, but he had a hood on that time. I'm sure it was the same guy. I'll never forget his gravelly voice. I guess he was sure he would succeed so he forgot the disguise."

"I wonder why he didn't just get on with it and shoot you when he walked in?" Alex voiced the question on his mind.

"This time he felt it necessary to explain why I had to die."

"And what was the reason?"

"When I tell you his name, you'll understand."

Alex was hooked, "Okay, what is it?"

"Bruce Smythe."

The name didn't immediately ring a bell with Alex, "Who?"

"Bruce Smythe. Perhaps you'll know when I tell you Eddie Smythe was my lover—before he disappeared, that is."

"I'm a little slow on the uptake. What happened to this guy Eddie?"

"He just stopped coming by," Judy answered, and a sad expression appeared on her face. "His brother told me he was the guy they found at the dump, burned up." Before Alex could answer, she continued, "The brother was sure my father had Eddie killed, for whatever reason. That's why he started the fire the first time he tried to kill me. He was sending a gruesome message."

"Did Vince do it?" Alex asked disbelievingly. He liked Judy's father, even though he knew the man had some rough edges.

"How do I know? I wouldn't put it past him, though. He didn't like Eddie, because he was paying attention to me." And she added, "Whatever Eddie was, he didn't deserve to die, not that way. At least now I know he didn't just dump me. I thought it was something I'd done."

Alex felt compelled to answer, "I don't think anyone in their right mind would walk away from you if you cared for them."

"What a nice thing to say. I think I'll keep you around," the statement was accompanied by a wide smile. "You've certainly brightened my day."

A uniformed policeman came into Judy's bedroom. He announced himself, "I'm Patrolman Stevens, Mister Chester. We're going to need you to come down to the station to get an eyewitness account of what happened here. Will you do that?"

"Sure," Alex answered. Privately he thought *Sergeant Helmand is going to love this*. "I've got something I need to do first," he said, thinking of Mary. "Can I come down in the morning?"

"If that's the best you can do, I'm sure it will be all right," the patrolman said cordially.

"Is Mr. Evans going to be okay?" Alex asked.

"I'm not sure. He lost a lot of blood, but the ambulance got here pretty quick."

"Where did they take him, do you know?"

"Yeah. He'll be at Mercy, down on Henderson. It's not too far from here, maybe two miles." The cop looked in the direction of Judy Graves, "Glad you're all right, miss. Looks like Mr. Chester here is your guardian angel."

She answered with a smile, "Guess I'll have to keep him around. I wonder if he takes care of traffic tickets?"

"That's my cue to get out of here. Try to get some sleep, Judy," Alex headed for the door, followed by the policeman Stevens.

"Hurry back," she said, and then mischievously, she added, "My love."

As Alex turned toward Mary's apartment, he encountered Jim Denton in the hallway.

"I see you're quite a celebrity," and he added, "again."

Alex wasn't in the mood for general conversation, so he answered, in a disinterested tone, "I just got there first," and brushed past the man.

Denton wasn't ready to let him go at that. He said, a little belligerently, "Just don't think you have the inside track to Mary. I'm in the race too."

"Good luck," he said, as he knocked on Mary's door.

There was no answer. Alex was about to walk away when he was approached by a man he didn't know. The stranger was looking at him as if to take in his features, perhaps so he could remember later. Alex was perplexed, not knowing what this man wanted.

"Can I help you?" he said.

The man finally spoke, "You look like someone I knew, a long time ago. The nose is different, and the clothes, but don't I know you?"

"I used to live here, in this apartment."

"Sure," the man said, "O'Bannion, isn't it? I was your neighbor."

"You're probably talking about my brother. I left to go to war in 1942, and I don't remember you."

"So I'm not going crazy."

Alex was confused, "What do you mean?"

"Was your brother's name Alan?"

"Still is, as far as I know. I've been looking for him, and the rest of my family. Can you help me?" For only the second time since he'd returned from the war, he was encouraged. Perhaps he would finally find them.

"I thought I heard them call you Mister Chester."

"I know it must be confusing, but believe me—the O'Bannions are my family, no matter what you've heard."

"They're gone, all of them."

"I know. I'm trying to find out where," Alex answered, becoming impatient.

"No, you don't understand. They're all dead. It happened about four years ago."

Two unrelated thoughts entered the mind of Alex O'Bannion at that instant, as his knees buckled and he almost fell. Maybe this guy is not telling the truth, and I've been looking in the wrong place.

The man was saying something, but Alex didn't hear. He was remembering. It was that last day when he was at the train station. They were holding each other close, and Emily whispered in his ear, as his mother and father stood nearby, "If you can't come back to me, we'll be together again somehow. I promise." It sounded cryptic at the time, and he'd let it go, saying nothing, but at that moment, in that time, he felt his wife really did love him. It had been touch and go for a while when he'd wondered if they were just living in a fantasy world.

He was jerked back to the present by the tone of the man's voice.

"I remember the date because it was my birthday. Your parents were coming to a party my wife was having later that evening. It was a terrible accident. They both died immediately. They were just out walking their dog. They were on the sidewalk, and the other driver, an old woman, jumped the curb with her big car. She never even went to jail. It was all in the paper the next day, except the trial, where all she got was probation. We canceled the party, of course."

"What was the date?"

"November 4th, 1948. I'll never forget. I turned 48 that day. You see, I was born at the turn of the century."

Not finding Mary at her apartment, Alex decided to get his interview with the police sergeant in charge of the Judy Graves case over with.

It was getting dark when he arrived at the station house. He had had such a jolt to his system with the news of his parents, and his wife and brother, that he'd lost track of time. The neighbor had gone on to relate the story of what happened to Emily and Alan. The end had come right there in the Alliant Arms, not long after the accident that claimed his parents. No wonder the super of the building—what was his name, Tony?—had panicked when he recognized Alex but mistook him for his brother Alan. He thought he was seeing a ghost. Had he not reacted the way he did, Tony could probably have told Alex the whole sordid story of the event that took his brother's life and the subsequent demise of his wife.

He was in luck. Sergeant Helmand was still there. His greeting was quite different than before. "There he is, the conquering hero," and he added, "again." He motioned for Alex to take a seat, across from his desk, "You have some penchant for getting in and out of trouble young man, but I'm glad to see you're none the worse for wear." As an afterthought, he said, "I think Miss Graves considers you her guardian angel."

Alex wished people wouldn't keep using that term, "So what did you want to see me about, Sergeant?"

"Well, at least you'll be glad to know we no longer consider you a suspect in the first attack," Helmand grinned. "If we'd figured out who her father was at the beginning of the investigation, this whole mess might have been solved sooner, and you wouldn't have been put in danger, not to mention the lady herself. It was pretty sloppy police work."

Alex was surprised the man would admit that. "It all worked out in the end, though. I'm just sorry Judy was scared out of her wits, and the reporter Evans was shot. How is he, by the way?"

"He'll survive. They had to give him a blood transfusion at the hospital. He'd lost a lot, but it could have been worse if you hadn't stemmed the flow from his neck. I haven't got the full report of his condition yet, but you might want to visit him. He's at Mercy, on the seventh floor, if they haven't moved him."

"I'll do that."

"Oh yeah," Helmand continued, "you still have to get your ID. I think we can do without it now, but for your own sake, carry it with you."

"Yes sir. Thanks."

"Thank you," Helmand answered, as he stood, signaling the end of the interview. Alex wasn't ready to go just yet, though.

"How did the bad guy get the police uniform?" It had been on his mind ever since the incident.

"That's easy," the sergeant answered, "He was a cop. He came from the north side. He sent our guy away for coffee, telling him he'd watch the place until the regular guard got back. I guess he figured out the dead guy on the trash heap was his brother before anyone else did, probably because he had disappeared. No one else was looking for this guy Eddie the Tuna so they didn't make the connection. We solved that case by the way. We just collared the shooter today. Funny, it was Vince Arrizano who clued us in. Seems the Tuna liked to play the horses, and he stiffed the bookie, who is a major player on the Northside. Eddie figured that since he worked for Arrizano, he was immune to being hassled. But then Vince cut him loose for some reason, and since the slob couldn't pay up, they took it out in trade, so to speak. That's the way things work in this city. We just wait long enough and the bad guys take care of themselves."

"I'll be damned."

"Yeah, so will Eddie," Helmand laughed at his own joke. "And you'll be happy to know his brother is safely behind bars and should be for a long time."

As Alex was leaving, he turned back toward the detective, "There was something else I wanted to ask you."

"Yes. What is it?"

"Somebody mentioned there was a murder in the apartments where my cousin lives. Do you know when that was?" He held his breath, hoping for a positive answer.

"I didn't work that case, but I remember it, because of the gruesomeness of it. It was right after New Year's, in 1949, I think. Time has a way of getting away from a person at this age. I do seem to remember that it was in the same apartment your cousin rents. Ironic huh?"

"Yeah." *You could say that again*, he thought. Almost as an afterthought, he asked another question. He hoped it would sound like he was just curious, and had no invested interest in the answer. "Do you know what happened to the woman?"

"I don't know. Like I said, I didn't work that case."

Alex was about to let it go, when Helmand continued, "The guy who did has the night shift. He'll be in at 11 pm. His name's Halloran."

Alex wanted to get down on his hands and knees and kiss the sergeant's hands, but he answered, "Thanks again, Sarge," as he went out the swinging doors, and down the steps to the street. There was a bounce to his gait that hadn't been there before.

Now Alex had a reference to check at the library, thanks to Detective Helmand. Hopefully, they'd have newspaper accounts of the murder, and maybe some clue as to what happened to his wife. If that didn't work out, he'd come back and see the detective after 11.

He suddenly realized he was tired, and decided to forego his trip to the library and the hospital, not to mention trying to find Mary. He'd waited long enough to settle things. Another day shouldn't matter.

He walked the short six blocks to the YMCA, his domicile of record lately. He wondered if he would ever be able to resolve things with Mary. He couldn't just leave it the way it was when last they'd seen each other. At least, he hoped not. There was a reason to settle their differences now. He was a single man if what the neighbor of Mary had told him was true. Maybe he'd find out for sure tomorrow.

The last thing on his mind before he fell asleep on his hard cot in the YMCA dorm was the way Mary had looked when he told her he wasn't free. There'd been something between them. He felt it, and he was sure she did too.

30

He awoke to a loud banging noise. At first, he forgot where he was, and he thought maybe Mary was in the kitchen getting ready for work. Then he remembered. The sound he heard must be the city waking up outside. It was time to begin his busy day too. He rose, put on the same clothes Mary had bought him, remembering that shopping should be on his list too. He found the head, washing his face in cold water to get the cobwebs out. He had no comb or other essentials, so he used a paper towel to dry his face and hair, thankful his hair was short enough he didn't need a comb. There was no mirror in the bathroom, probably because of the clientele, and the fear it would just be broken.

When he felt he was ready, he decided his first stop should be the library, after he found a restaurant for breakfast. He still had quite a bit of the money Vince Arrizano had paid him to babysit his daughter and change her wounds.

So much depended on what he learned from old newspapers that he wanted to get that out of the way before checking on Blake Evans at the hospital. The fact the library was the closest to the Y was also a consideration. He would have to ride the El or catch a cab to get to the hospital.

Besides, visiting hours were probably after 10 am. The library should be open at 9 am. He'd forgotten his watch in Judy's bedroom again, understandably, with all that had gone on there. Luckily there was a clock on the wall at the Y, so he knew he had time to eat, get to the library shortly after 9 am, and still make it to the hospital by 10 am. Surely Judy would be home that evening so he could at least pick up his watch. With any luck, he'd do more than that while he was at the Alliant Arms, now that it seemed he was a free man, at least where Emily was concerned. He did have mixed feelings regarding the two women. He certainly didn't want to find out his wife was no longer among the living, but on the other side of the coin, he definitely had feelings for the little redhead he'd known for such a short while.

Things were falling into place on this day. He did wonder where Mary had been through. She might not even know what had happened down the hall from her place. He didn't have her phone number or he might have called her. He could call information, but having to use a payphone was inconvenient. He decided it would be better to see her in person for what he wanted to say.

A different lady was at the information desk when he arrived. She was younger. He nodded to her as he passed by. This time he knew where to find things.

He located the paper racks and quickly found the 1949 issues. He began with the first day of the New Year. After about an hour of browsing, when he determined it would take longer than he thought, he became worried he might not make the morning visiting hours at the hospital. He hoped they would go till noon. He should be able to get there before that. If they shut down at 11 or 11:30 am, he might have to postpone till the afternoon. That would be inconvenient, but necessary. He really wanted to check on Evans. He felt somewhat responsible for the reporter's condition. If they hadn't broken into Judy's place, he wouldn't have been shot. Of course, the woman would most likely be dead. No one wanted that to be the outcome…except for the killer. That reminded Alex, he needed to change her bandages before the day was over. He wondered if her father would want some of his money back, now that the danger to her had passed. He might be out of a job.

There it was! The article he was looking for. It was on the front page of the paper. The headline read: GRUESOME MURDER ON THE SOUTH SIDE. It went on to detail the events of that day, January fifth. Most of it Alex already knew from Mary and Judy's neighbor. The article just verified it. The neighbor had said Emily was dead too. Alex wondered where he could check that. It would be in the papers somewhere but God knows where. Maybe the information lady would know something about it. She might be too young, but the other one, the lady who'd been at the desk before, could remember.

Feeling a little letdown, since all the information he wanted was not readily available, Alex headed for the hospital. Since time was becoming a problem, he hailed a cab. Luckily the driver wasn't interested in small talk. Alex would just as soon be left with his own considerable problems. He wasn't equipped to help anyone else with theirs.

He paid the fare, with a small tip, and headed up to the seventh floor of the hospital. At the nurse's station, he learned that Blake Evans was indeed there, and in room 713. When he entered the room, it was quiet. He thought maybe the reporter was sleeping, but his eyes were wide open.

The man in the bed reached out his hand to Alex when his visitor came close to where he lay covered with a sheet up to his shoulders. Still, there was no sound coming from the wounded man's lips.

Alex took his hand, and with a perplexed look on his face, he said, "What's going on, Evans? Can't you talk?"

With that, the man in the bed pointed to something on the table next to where he lay. There was a clipboard with a pencil and paper attached. Suddenly, Alex got it. The guy couldn't talk, even if he wanted to.

He handed the clipboard to him, and when Evans again pointed to the side of his bed, Alex cranked it up so the bedridden man wouldn't be completely prone. He was getting the hang of this silent movie.

After writing something on the paper, he handed it to Alex. He had written, "I can't talk because my voice box was nicked by the bullet."

"Oh, no. I'm really sorry. If we hadn't broken, in you'd be all right," Alex knew that sounded dumb, but he couldn't think of anything else at that moment.

Blake motioned for the clipboard again. This time, he wrote, "It's supposed to heal so I can talk." There was more, "You saved my life."

Alex had no trouble finding words to answer that, "I was trying to save mine."

"How did you? I passed out," were the next words on a second sheet of paper. Alex went on to explain what happened and that everyone was all right, except for the gunman, who was safely in jail where he belonged.

Blake Evans again reached for the hand of the man he knew as Joe Chester, after writing in large letters, "THANK YOU."

31

Jim Denton was the one let go by Judy's father. He didn't like it, but he agreed the threat to his daughter had been resolved. He decided to remain at the Alliant Arms anyway, at least for a while. He was attracted to both Mary Abrams and Judy Graves. He couldn't deny that. He'd been flirtatious early on, but that was just his nature when he encountered a pretty woman. Hell, Mary and Judy were both good looking. Besides, moving was always a hassle.

He'd hung around the hallway after his confrontation with Joe Chester, long enough to know Mary didn't answer her door. He wondered at the time where she might have gone. Or perhaps she anticipated it was the Marine on the other side, and she didn't want to talk to him. Denton hoped that was the case.

He'd even toyed with the idea of turning Chester in. He knew that wasn't his real name. The proof the guy was AWOL was hanging in Mary's closet, along with the helmet and boots. There wasn't any navy or Marine Corps office there in Chicago, save the recruiting stations, but the Great Lakes Naval Training Station wasn't too far north. Surely, they'd be interested in what he knew.

Still, he hesitated. The man going by the name Chester wasn't really a bad guy, just a competitor. He didn't deserve to spend the next few years in jail. Or did he? Where had he been before showing up on Mary's doorstep? Denton wondered if there was any way he could check on that. Then there was the uniform. It didn't look like what the Marines were wearing in Korea, at least from images he'd seen on TV newscasts. It was more like the movies he'd seen depicting World War Two battles. That was strange, to say the least.

Suddenly, an idea came to him. If he could get into Mary's apartment, he could take part of the uniform from her closet, and then carry it up to the training center for analysis. He could make up some story about finding it and just being curious. Maybe he'd even take the helmet too. That way he'd have an answer, which he could tell Mary, and get back in her good graces, even after stealing stuff from her apartment. She would understand that he was just looking after her welfare. Chester could be a thief or murderer for all she knew. Hell, he might even be a communist.

He made up his mind to go through with his plan, with one variation. He would take the uniform to the FBI right there in Chicago.

He went to Mary's door and knocked. Maybe she'd come home late the evening before.

There was no answer. Disappointed, he walked back to his own apartment to wait it out. Surely, she would be home soon. That day was a workday for most. He knew for a fact she had the weekends off. This being Monday, she should be home late in the afternoon.

Driving back from Indiana by herself, Mary had plenty of time to think. She'd gone to her parents' house to get some advice, but she didn't like what she'd heard. She admonished herself silently. She should have known better.

She'd had a week's vacation, and she would have stayed the full time if she hadn't gotten so mad. As it was, it only took one night to drive her out of that house. She would save the last five days she was to have had off by returning to work on Wednesday.

Everything was fine at first. When her folks recognized her car, they rushed out to greet her, smiling broadly. They gushed over her, while her mom fixed supper, and her dad put away his paper to give her his full attention. After a traditional meat and potatoes meal, they moved from the dining room into the living room to relax and let their food digest. That's when the conversation drifted into confrontational territory.

Her dad as usual had picked out the beige recliner to stretch out in. His newspaper was on the table next to him but he didn't reach for it. Instead, he looked across the room at his daughter and asked, as much to start the conversation as anything, "How's your love life, honey?"

"Daddy, I don't have a love life, that's why I'm here," she giggled.

"Oh, that's nice," he answered, obviously not having heard a word she said.

Her father wasn't really the one she wanted to confide in, anyway. He always agreed with her mother. "Read your paper, Daddy. Mom and I have to have a serious conversation."

He heard that, and dutifully picked up the paper, placing it between himself and his wife.

"Okay. Mom, I met someone," Mary leaned forward toward her mother as she spoke as if it was a sacred secret only she and her mother were sharing.

"That's good sweetheart. You are 19. I was 14 when I married your father. I've never regretted it."

Mary knew that wasn't true. She could remember when she was 13. Her mom actually kicked her dad out of the house. He'd come home drunk from an office party, and he could hardly stand up. She asked him how much he'd had to drink and he'd lied, saying only a couple of beers. Then he tried to kiss her to smooth it over, and the smell of the alcohol almost made her nauseous. She had taken his hand and led him to the front door, saying, "Don't come back in this house until you're sober. Your breath stinks and your clothes reek of bourbon."

He had left, and he didn't come back until the next day after work. Her mother asked him where he'd spent the night, and he answered he'd slept at his office. He was an accountant, and he had an office all to himself. In a testament to the truth of what he said, he was wearing the same clothes. Some of what she had told him must have gotten through though, for his clothes no longer smelled of alcohol. He must have washed them somewhere. But a strange thing happened. From that time on, Mary never knew her father to drink, or disagree with anything his wife said.

"There's a problem. He's married."

Her mother, who hardly ever raised her voice, literally shouted, "Then you must break it off." There was no room for discussion in her tone.

"Wait, Mom, you haven't heard the whole story."

"I don't need to. There'll be nothing but misery for you if you don't leave him."

"How can I leave him if we haven't been together?"

"What do you mean?"

Mary was remembering, "We were dancing, and I wanted to move closer because I really care for this guy. He held me back, saying he was married."

"Darling, you have your whole life ahead of you. You'll meet lots of men to choose from. Don't waste your time on someone who's not available."

It was like her mother was closed off. There was no room for discussion. In her defense, she didn't know the whole story. Even Mary didn't. But the fact that her mother had just dismissed any further discussion on the matter, though typical of the woman, infuriated her. Over her mother's objections, she said she remembered something she had forgotten to do in Chicago, and walked out. Her father didn't even see her.

Mary realized on the trip back to the city that there were many things she didn't know about the man she had fallen in love with, but she was going to find out.

32

What kind of man am I? Alex was thinking. *I'm actually excited about the possibility my marriage no longer exists.* He should be paying homage to the woman he married. In his mind, it wasn't that long ago that he had said in sickness and health, and a few other words, to his childhood sweetheart, words that supposedly sealed their future together.

It had been inevitable they would marry. Emily had been his next-door neighbor from the time they were in grammar school. She was his confidante. He was 14 when he tried smoking and got sick because of it. His folks thought he had the flu, but he only told Emily what it really was. She admonished him like a parent, and he didn't smoke again until boot camp in the Marines. Everyone smoked then.

Emily was growing into a beautiful woman before his eyes, but he didn't notice, not for a long time. Both of them were the same age, with birthdays only a month apart. She was 16 when he finally saw her as someone other than the tomboy next door.

It happened suddenly, and was a surprise to Alex. Another boy who had been interested in Emily made a disparaging comment about her one day, and Alex had defended her physically. He won the fight but received a broken nose in the process. It didn't look too bad, and he didn't tell his mom and dad about the encounter. By the time they realized the nose was broken, it would have been extremely painful to have it reset, and Alex had no trouble breathing, so they did nothing. The fight awakened Alex to the fact that he cared more about Emily than he had thought. From then on, their relationship took on a new meaning.

It was an exciting time for them both. Certainly, it began as puppy love, but to them, it was the real thing. They shivered at the touch of their partner. Their world was suddenly a vibrant, happy garden where all the colors around them seemed brighter. It was enough just to hold hands on most times. Neither of them had to vocalize their feelings. They just knew.

When Emily's mother was sent away to a hospital, it was Alex who consoled the distraught girl. They were only 17. When the days dragged on, and Emily cried at night as it became apparent something was terribly wrong with her mother, it was Alex who was there for her. He often slept on the couch at her house, reluctant to be away if she cried out for him.

They were married shortly after they both turned 20, with her father's blessing, and his parents' reluctant agreement.

It was about that time the elder O'Bannions moved into the Alliant Arms. Alex and Emily were staying with her father over in Fairfield.

Everything went well for a while. They didn't have a lot of money, but they didn't need much, living with her father.

On the few times the young marrieds went out to a movie, they were able to borrow her father's old Ford coupe.

By late 1941, Emily was becoming restless. When Alex's twin brother Alan would come to visit, she found him more interesting than her husband. He was so much more outgoing. While Alex was content just relaxing at home with a beer and his newspaper, Emily wanted to go out. Once in a while, Alan convinced his brother to let him escort her to a movie, or out for coffee, just to get out of the house. It was a recipe for disaster as far as the marriage was concerned.

At the same time, Emily's father became interested in another woman. His wife was incarcerated in a sanitarium with visions of monsters and evil people trying to harm her. It was time for the young O'Bannions to move. They moved in with his parents at the Alliant Arms, where his father and mother moved to a larger apartment to accommodate the couple who couldn't yet afford to get a place of their own.

Then came the war. Alex and Emily weren't getting along that well, and the now 20-year-old received his draft notice. He joined the Marines instead, without telling Emily his intentions. She was furious, but the damage was done, so to speak. He left a week later for boot camp, after passing his physical at the Great Lakes Naval Training Center.

At first, Emily's letters arrived regularly. He reciprocated. The words on paper were reminiscent of those they had recited earlier in the days shortly before, and for a while after their marriage. Then came deployment, and Guadalcanal.

33

While waiting for Mary to return so he could put his plan into operation, Jim Denton wandered down the hall to the apartment of Judy Graves. He hadn't seen her since she'd almost been killed. When he knocked on her door, he was surprised to hear her cheerful voice yell, "Come in." When he opened the unlocked door, he received his second shock. She was in her kitchen preparing some kind of meal. She was wearing a long flowing pink robe with big open sleeves, and she looked as if she'd just stepped out of a magazine advertisement.

"Wow," he said, obviously impressed with the vision of her. "To hear everyone else in the building tell it, I thought you were on the verge of death."

"Hi, Jim. Long time no see," she answered cheerfully. "Have you eaten? I could use the company. No one's been to see me for almost a day."

"What are you fixing? I'm really picky," he teased. It was good to see her up and about, even if it was only to the kitchen.

"It's an omelet, and you'll love it or else."

As he walked over to her kitchen table and sat down on one of the wooden chairs, he said, "How long have you been up?"

She brought plates and silverware to the table, "You mean this morning? Only about an hour or so. I really had a good night's sleep, for a change." She reached down to her stomach and continued, "My burns didn't hurt at all. Joe really did a good job cleaning and tending to them." She noticed that Jim had a frown on his face, and she realized he didn't want to hear about another man. *Guys are strange,* she thought to herself. Then she wondered where her savior was. She hadn't seen him in over 24 hours.

Jim Denton got even, "Do you know where Mary Abrams is? She hasn't been around for a day or so."

"No, love. People in this building don't wander through my apartment on their way down the hall."

"Funny," he said, "I just hope nothing's happened to her. Strange things have a way of seeking out this building."

"Boy, you can say that again."

He started to, but she stopped him, "I was being rhetorical." She didn't know what that meant, but it sounded good. She smiled. It was really good to have someone to talk to. At least he hadn't made a pass at her yet. She just wished it was Joe sitting at her table. *Where is he?* she thought.

Alex realized something when he woke up that morning. It would be a perfect opportunity to stop by Mary's place. He really wanted to talk to her, to tell her what he'd learned about his family, especially his wife. *Wait a minute*, he thought, *she's not my wife anymore.* It was morbid, but it was true. To verify it, he had decided the night

152

before, while searching for sleep on the hard cot they called beds, to chance to stop by Tony Angelo's apartment to ask him the full story. If he could calm the man down, he might learn for sure what happened to Emily. He'd called the police station, and the cop named Halloran was off that night.

First, he had to get some clothes and shaving accessories. He was getting a full beard and it was beginning to itch. It would be nice to have a comb too. As his hair was growing, it was harder to smooth it down with only his hands.

After dressing in the soiled clothes Mary had gotten him so many days ago and washing his face, he headed for a department store. He didn't want to go to Woolworth's for fear Mary might be there and see him in less than his best.

He found a Kress' a few blocks from the Y. He bought some slacks, a couple of collared shirts, socks, shoes, black this time, and even a tie. He went back to the YMCA to change, found a locker to store his other garments, and headed for the Alliant Arms.

Mary was late getting into town, just after midnight. She set her alarm for 7 am before retiring. The next day was a workday if she wanted. She was still on vacation so they weren't expecting her. Still, she needed something to occupy her mind, other than her feelings for the Marine who had swept into her life less than a month ago and somehow stolen her heart.

It wasn't as if she were desperate for a man. She'd had lots of dates, and there was a guy in her own building who was interested. She didn't know what it was about Alex O'Bannion that continued to occupy her mind. Maybe it was because he was a hero, and therefore dashing, but she didn't think so. It could be that he was so lost, that made him appealing. It didn't hurt that he was extremely handsome, except his nose. Perhaps it was all those things that made her picture him in the proverbial rose-colored cottage, by a fire, with a pipe, and a couple of little ones romping around—hers, of course. *My God, snap out of it, girl. He's taken.*

By the time Alex reached the apartments, he had decided how to approach the building super. He would knock softly, then step back so he wouldn't be right in the guy's face to scare him. It worked, or at least something did. Tony Angelo was very calm when he opened the door to Alex's knock. It seems he realized it was Alex and not his dead brother Alan confronting him. He did indeed know what had become of Emily O'Bannion. He related the story to Alex, of how she was so troubled and ended up on the streets after she was prematurely released from jail. It was such a sad story, Tony said, as he was remembering. Such a pretty young lady too.

Alex felt as if a heavy weight had been removed from his neck as he literally bounded up the stairs on his way to Mary's apartment. Then he remembered he had been neglecting Judy Graves, so he stopped by her apartment first.

When he knocked, he heard a man's voice from inside saying, "I'll get that." He knew it wasn't Judy's father because he didn't have that deep, gravelly pitch. Suddenly, he was face to face with Jim Denton.

"What are you doing here?" they each said, almost in unison.

154

"I was worried about Judy. How about you?" Denton answered.

"Same. I haven't changed her bandages in over a day now," Alex couldn't see Judy from where he was standing, still in the hall.

"I was wondering where you were," it was Judy, speaking loudly from the kitchen table.

He stepped inside, forcing Denton to move back. "You're up," he said, with a surprised tone to his voice.

"And doing very well, no thanks to you," she wasn't going to let him off the hook just yet.

"I'm sorry Judy, I had so much going on, it just slipped my mind. Do you think your dad will fire me?"

Before Judy could answer, Jim Denton piped up, "No, he saved that for me."

"What do you mean?" Alex was confused.

Denton decided it was time to come clean, "You didn't know, but Arrizano senior hired me to watch out for Judy, even before the attack on her. I'm a private detective. He found out somehow that I lived here, and what I did for a living, maybe by calling my office and talking to Mabel."

"Who's Mabel?" they both asked in unison.

"My secretary."

Both Judy and Alex were surprised. Judy spoke first. "So you've been lying to me all this time. I thought you were just interested in me."

"Well, I was, kind of. I'm certainly not interested in Mabel. She's 62 years old. It was a perk of the job, you being so beautiful and all," he hoped that would get him off the hook.

It seemed to work. She smiled.

155

"At least your eyesight is okay," Alex broke in.

"You're both full of it. Now, why not vacate the premises so I can get some rest. This cooking has tired me out." She wasn't really weary. She just couldn't handle the two of them right then, even with the flattery.

Once out in the hall, Alex asked Denton, "Have you seen Mary this morning? I need to talk to her."

"No, but I haven't checked this morning," he said as they both walked down to her door.

It was a little awkward for Alex. He really wanted to see Mary alone, to tell her what he'd learned since last he'd seen her. Still, he knocked on her door. There was no answer.

34

By the time their plane landed on Guadalcanal, the group had quite a reputation. In addition to the good work they'd done on Oahu in the Hawaiian Islands, they found three Marines and two sailors in Guam that had been listed as missing in action. It was strange, really. All of these guys were alive and kicking, so to speak. They had married island girls, and just abandoned their military careers, without telling anyone. They didn't think it would hurt since the war was over. They would have just been mustered out, anyway. Two of the women were actually sisters.

When Washington was notified, they chose to ignore it. The new President was taking all their time in the transition. He'd just been elected the week before the news reached the mainland.

Oliver West was raring to go when they deplaned. The others in the party wanted to find their living quarters and freshen up. He excused himself and went off on his own.

His first stop, after landing at Honiara—the largest town of the biggest island in the Solomons—was the military cemetery. They had arrived at 1 pm in the afternoon, so he only had half a day before dark to explore the northern part of the island. His action in 1942 had taken place there, anyway.

As one might expect, the quietness of the hallowed site was interrupted only by the sound of the breeze rustling the palms, which surrounded the cemetery on all sides. Oliver had the place to himself, except for the ghosts of friends who had fallen while in his company. They filled his mind, and he briefly found himself back in time, when they were advancing toward the airfield.

He walked among the rows of crude crosses, and read the scribbling of names on each. By the time darkness overtook him, he had only covered about half of the section. There were many names he recognized, but not the one he had come to find. He didn't really expect to locate the final resting place of Private Alex O'Bannion, but there had been a chance.

There were no lights to illuminate the area, so Oliver reluctantly decided to continue the search after what he hoped was a good night's sleep. He just barely beat the malaria-carrying mosquitoes back to the hotel where his group was billeted. He had forgotten the disease-carrying insects that had wreaked havoc among the troops not that long ago.

The next morning he was back at the cemetery, almost before dawn. It would be noon before he had completed his journey through the entire graveyard. He was glad he'd come but disappointed he'd come up empty, as far as the one name that would have made it all worthwhile.

It finally occurred to the reserve major that he hadn't eaten since breakfast the previous day, and that was a small meal on the aircraft before landing at Henderson Field on

Lunga Point. He'd been so occupied with his itinerary and memories of the battles fought there, food didn't enter his cluttered mind.

He found a Melanesian restaurant in town and went inside. He was surprised to see a Japanese waiter, who was heading in his direction after he was seated off in a corner of the establishment. Then he realized that, just as in Guam, some of the expatriates just didn't return home when the war ended. If the man had been a soldier, he must have hidden out until the invading Americans left the island for good. Of course, he could have just returned after the war. Some of the Japs had escaped when it became apparent in 1943 they had lost.

It was unreal, watching the man, an apron around his waist, walking toward Oliver's table. This was a civilized setting, where it was just the opposite before. There was no civilization, only men in battle dress, killing before being erased from that uncivil jungle. Had it only been ten years? It seemed like an eternity. Now it was as if it never happened at all. Yet men had lost their dreams of a future, men of both sides. Women had forever lost their soulmates, children, and their fathers.

"I help you please?" the attendant muttered in pidgin English, obviously as uncomfortable as his patron seated before him. This man could have easily been his enemy back then, waiting for him undercover, machine gun at the ready.

"Do you have a menu?" Oliver asked, pronouncing each word slowly.

The waiter walked away without answering. In another minute, he came back, carrying a thin sheet of paper, which he handed to West. Oliver was relieved when he noticed the menu was in both the local language and English. A hamburger and fries were even listed.

"I'll have this," he said, pointing to the American food. The waiter said nothing but wrote something on his pad. "I want a beer too," Oliver continued. He didn't care what brand and the attendant didn't ask, as he walked away.

When his food arrived, along with his beer, Oliver asked the same waiter, "Were you in the war?"

The man, who looked to be in his early thirties, nodded and said, "Hai."

"Were you there when the airfield was attacked by the Americans?"

The waiter hesitated, but then answered, "Hai." He looked around the restaurant, hoping someone needed him, for he felt uncomfortable discussing the war with this American. Unfortunately, all the patrons seemed to be doing well.

"The war's over man, I'm just making conversation," Oliver could see the waiter's discomfort. "I was there too, on the other side," he had stated the obvious.

Again the man answered, "Hai." He seemed to relax some.

"I'm here trying to find out what happened to a missing Marine. He disappeared during that battle," Oliver felt telling this waiter why he had come was a futile gesture, but it was like handing someone your business card. Maybe they would say I'm interested in that.

"Oh. Sorry. I do not know anything about that."

Oliver was surprised the man answered in English, but he was even more bewildered by his body language. He had shifted feet nervously, and some perspiration showed on his forehead.

"I go now. Customers need me," he backed away and almost stumbled against another table behind him.

Oliver was bothered enough by the waiter's reaction that he asked the cashier, after paying his bill, if he knew the name of the man who had waited on him.

She answered, smiling, "He is Kyoto Shigera. Very good worker. Speak perfect English. We call him Willie."

35

It had been two days since Alex last saw Mary. She didn't know what he'd found out. He wished she'd given him a key, but neither of them had thought of that when she first decided to let him bunk there.

He was anxious to share his news. Maybe it would make a difference in their relationship. He was certainly ready. His loneliness had made him feel so isolated from everything. But he had felt the need to push Mary away when they both knew there was something between them, other than the secret they shared.

He wondered if the uniform was still hanging in her closet. It wouldn't do for anyone to find it. They would want answers he couldn't supply. He didn't know how he got back to Chicago from the war zone, or what had happened to him in the ten years he couldn't account for. He wondered if he would ever know.

Once out on the street, he decided to circle back. He could hang out at Judy's to wait for Mary. That wasn't exactly fair to the wounded girl, but he did want to check her burns, and apply more salve, even though she obviously felt better, well enough to get out of bed.

He decided to knock on her door, rather than just walk in as he'd had to do when she was bedridden.

He heard nothing as he stood there outside her door. *She couldn't be away*, he thought. *She's not that much recovered that she can gadabout. Maybe Smythe had an accomplice.* A chill spread over his body.

The door opened, and there she stood. She was adorned in a one-piece beige short-sleeve dress. Her brown hair was done up in a bun, and she was wearing make-up. Her lipstick was a light shade of like a burnt red, almost between red and brown. It went with her dress, and she looked good.

Alex stood there, his mouth agape. "Where do you think you're going?" was all he could think of to say.

"I just need to get some air," she answered, "I've been cooped up here too long."

He could tell she wasn't wearing anything under her dress up top, as her nipples pushed against the fabric. He had mixed feelings about that. It was very provocative to be sure, but it was probably more comfortable where her burns were concerned. He hoped that was the reason she dressed that way.

"Don't push your recovery. You don't want a relapse." What he really felt was that he didn't want to get too close to this babe and cloud his judgment. She was a knockout, to be sure.

"Oh," she pouted, "you're no fun." Then she amended that, "At least, not now." She was remembering his gentle hands on her as he applied the salve to her burns.

"I came to give you one more treatment. Can we get this over with? I've got things to do," changing the subject was one of them.

"Oh, all right," and she took his hand, leading him into her bedroom.

Vince Arrizano was upset. He'd just gotten word the Federal Government was indicting him for racketeering. It was too bad, really. He'd been shifting most of his operations into legit businesses. Now, it looked like he was going the route of Capone and others who had chosen the shady side of commerce.

He had to tell Judy. She was his only living relative and heir. He drove his black Lincoln to her place, parking on the street. Normally his bodyguard would accompany him, but since this was a personal call, and he had no idea how long he would stay with his daughter, he chose to take the car himself.

His lawyer, who had broken the news about the grand jury, told him he wouldn't have to report to the court for a couple of weeks, so there was time to arrange his affairs.

As he pulled up in front of the Alliant Arms, he failed to notice the Cadillac across the street, or the two men just sitting there, waiting for something.

He went up the stairs, thinking, *this is my daily exercise.* When he got to Judy's door, he didn't knock; he just walked in. Alex had made sure they left the bedroom door open, and Vince saw them in there. Luckily, Alex didn't have his hands on her right then. It wouldn't have been a pretty sight for any father.

"Hi, kids. I've been looking for you Joe, I've got those documents you wanted. They're in the car parked outside. When you finish with my daughter's treatment, maybe we can go get them?"

"Sure," Alex answered, "I'm almost finished here."

Judy piped in, "Go get yourself a beer out of the fridge, Dad. Joe's making love to me with his hands, and you don't want to see it," she teased, making Alex extremely uncomfortable.

"Careful kid," Vince retorted, "I'm packing." And he smiled. Truth be told, he felt his daughter could do worse than this good-looking guy.

It was about 15 minutes later that Vince Arrizano and Alex walked down to the street. Vince had not said a word to either of them about the verdict of the grand jury. When they reached the Lincoln, the car that had been parked across the street suddenly roared to life and made a U-turn just beyond the Lincoln. Both Vince and Alex noticed a barrel of a shotgun protruding from the passenger side window opening. Alex shoved a frozen Vince to the ground, falling on top of him just as a double-barreled blast rang out. They'd been standing by the trunk of Vince's car, but they ended up face down to the sidewalk as the Cadillac sped away. People came running out of the apartment as Alex lifted Vince to his feet. Neither of them had been hit, but the Lincoln sported a few new holes.

36

Bill Helmand was perplexed, to say the least. Why did all the action in the city have to happen in his district? When the call came in, he was in the John. Of course, no one else jumped up and said I'll take this one. They knew good old reliable Bill would be back in a minute and he'd beg for the case. That's the way he felt, anyway. He was in complete relaxation for a whole three minutes.

"You'll never believe what just happened," the officer on the incoming desk proclaimed when he emerged from his three-minute vacation.

"I got an early pension," Helmand replied, knowing that wasn't it. "What was it, really?"

"Vince Arrizano almost got whacked," and he chuckled. "It was in your district." There were three officers within earshot, and they laughed in unison.

"What happened?" the cop in him reappeared, and he was ready to work the case.

"He was ambushed down on Lincoln Street. He would have bought it if a bystander hadn't shoved him out of the line of fire."

"You say Lincoln Street. What address?" he was thinking that had to be close to the Alliant Arms.

"It was out front of the Graves' building. You know, where that fire was. I went there with you right after."

"Yeah. I remember. Okay, I'll head over there, unless one of you guys want it." Silence.

By the time he arrived, the beat cops had dispersed the crowd. They'd already taken reports from anyone who said they witnessed the shooting, which was exactly two. Those people—a man and a woman, looking to be in their seventies or older—were standing against the building. Vince Arrizano was sitting on the curb next to a Lincoln that obviously had taken a beating in its rear end. Next to him, but standing, was the man he knew as Joe Chester.

"Okay Mister Arrizano, what happened?" Helmand began.

"Do you know about the indictment against me?"

"No. Who indicted you?"

"The Feds. They're trying to prove racketeering, whatever that means."

Helmand shuffled his feet before answering. He wished they were at the station, "It means you're going to jail. Don't pass go. Don't collect 200 dollars." It was an obvious reference to the board game Monopoly.

Arrizano reacted, "Smart. How about catching the slobs who targeted me?"

"Okay. What can you tell me about them?"

"Hell, not much. I took a nosedive to the sidewalk. Why not ask the guy who pushed me and saved my life?"

"And who might that be?" he was sure he knew the answer since Chester was standing right there, but he wanted Arrizano to officially tell him, for the record.

Vince decided he could be cute too, "Let me introduce my guardian angel." He pointed toward Alex. As Helmand turned toward Alex, Vince walked over to his Lincoln.

As he reached for the lever to open the trunk, Helmand saw him and stepped away from Alex, yelling, "What the hell do you think you're doing?" obviously directing his wrath at the man standing in the street.

"I just need to get an envelope from my car," Vince answered as he pulled on the trunk handle.

"Stop! You can't get in there and remove anything. That car is being impounded."

"It's just an envelope. What's the big deal?"

"Everything relating to that Lincoln is part of the crime scene. It can't be removed until the forensic guys are done with it."

"Shit!" he retorted while slamming the trunk lid back down. He walked over to Alex and said quietly, "Sorry kid. I'll have to get it for you later."

Helmand could hear them talking, but couldn't hear what was being said. "You'll be notified when the crime guys are done with your car, and you'll be able to come to pick it up. For now, it'll be towed to the police lot."

"Yeah, great," Vince replied.

Mary was really weary when her shift ended. She'd been standing all day waiting on customers, except for the half-hour she'd had for lunch. She hadn't remembered to fix anything at home so she went to the lunch counter at the store and ordered a ham sandwich on toast. One of her coworkers sat next to her and asked how her weekend had gone. Mary just said it was fine, but it got her thinking about her confrontation with her mother. It seemed they always argued when they saw each other.

That question also made her think about Alex O'Bannion. She wished she hadn't been so short with him. It might be he was gone from her life forever. She made a mental note to check her closet when she got home, to see if his uniform was still there. She doubted he'd take it with him unless he was going to turn himself in to the authorities. She hoped that wasn't the case. He'd been AWOL for ten years, through no fault of his own, but that wouldn't count for much with the government, she was sure.

It was strange how Mary believed him when he told her he couldn't remember anything. He'd been in the jungle on that God-forsaken island, and then he wasn't. Where was he all that time? She didn't even know where they could check.

Wait a minute, she thought. *There is no we. He's gone.* For some reason, tears came to her eyes.

"Are you all right?" her coworker asked, putting down her soup spoon.

"Yes, I'm just tired. I'll probably take a nap when I get off work today." *If I can get that Marine off my mind.* She didn't say that.

Mary made a decision then that she would use the rest of her vacation after all. Her mind was so cluttered, she wasn't prepared to think about work just then. She notified her floor manager and received permission.

Vince didn't have a ride after they towed his car away, so Sergeant Helmand offered to take him home after he questioned the two witnesses. Vince declined, thinking it would be just too weird riding in the back of a police car, even if it was unmarked. He decided instead to try to bum a ride from Jim Denton, who used to be in his employ. He hoped the guy didn't harbor a grudge.

Denton was one of the people who had come to watch what was happening, and he had lingered not far away out of curiosity. Vince had seen him there, and that's where he got the idea to hit the P.I. up for a ride.

Vince asked Alex if he wanted to come with them and see his place, but Alex declined. He had nowhere to be, but he just wanted to wait for Mary to come home from work. He had to bridge the gap between them.

37

When Mary walked down the hall to her apartment that afternoon, there sat Alex, legs crossed, in front of her door. When she saw him, her pace quickened, though she didn't realize it. Then she noticed his eyes were closed, and he seemed to be sleeping. She stopped in front of him and studied his face. He seemed so peaceful. He'd never been that way until now. His face had seemed strained, with lines around his eyes making him look older. Now, here in the semi-darkened hallway, he appeared to be the same age as her. He was even more handsome to her if that was possible.

If she could have reached over him and unlocked her door without waking him, that's what she would have done. He must have needed the sleep. Spontaneously, she whispered, "I love you."

He stirred but didn't awaken. Finally, because she was tired, and she had nowhere else to go, she spoke his name. He moved slightly but remained asleep. She shook his shoulder. This time, his eyes flew open, and he reached for something that wasn't there, jumping up at the same time. Then, as his eyes focused, he saw Mary.

"I'm sorry, Mary. I must have been dreaming."

"What were you dreaming about?" she said, curious as to what would make him react like that.

"I was back in the jungle. I saw a Jap not 20 feet away from me. He was just standing there with his rifle at his side. He saw me, but still, he didn't raise the gun. I couldn't shoot, even though I knew I should. Then he raised his weapon and I could see a puff of smoke coming from the barrel, but I felt nothing. Then you woke me."

"Why don't we go inside? You'll be more comfortable." As she said it, she unlocked the door. Suddenly, she wasn't as tired.

"Did you just come from work?" Alex asked.

"Uh-huh. It's been a long day. I got home late last night, and couldn't get to sleep right away."

"I was thinking of you too," he anticipated her. "Where were you all weekend?"

"I went to visit my conscience."

"What?" he obviously didn't understand what she was saying.

"I went home to see my folks. I told them about you."

"Did you tell them everything?"

"No. How could I? I don't even understand it."

They were standing in the living room. Mary kicked off her heels, dropping about three inches. She stepped toward him and looking up, spoke softly, "Am I crazy for loving you?"

Once again, Alex put out his arms, stopping her, "How could you love me? You don't know anything about me."

Tears came to her eyes, and she said, "I don't know what it is if it's not love. I think of you all the time, and I worry that you might not be safe. I imagine you holding me, and telling me not to worry."

"Are you sure you're not just lonely?"

Mary walked over and sat on her sofa, "It's not that. I'm sure of it."

Suddenly wanting to be close to her, Alex came and sat next to her, "We hardly know each other. I want to know everything about you, and I want to share my life with you, so you have an idea who I really am."

"Who are you, Alex?"

"I was a clumsy kid. You wouldn't have even looked at me when I was in grade school."

Mary felt compelled to answer, "I find that very hard to believe."

"I was. I tried to be an athlete so the girls would like me, but it didn't work. They would see me coming and go the other way. I didn't even have a date for the senior prom."

"Oh. That's sad. I wish I had known you then. I would have asked you to the prom," she took his hand. He didn't pull away.

"Tell me about you. Did you have lots of boyfriends in high school?"

"I had a few. I was just trying to keep up appearances, though. They didn't mean anything to me. There was one guy though, that I was crazy about. That's because I wasn't really grown up yet."

"I'm jealous. I don't want to hear about him. Do you have any siblings?"

"I have two younger sisters."

"Where are they now?"

"I think they are still in Indiana. We aren't very close. I don't know why. They don't live at home with my parents. My youngest sister Evelyn moved out when she graduated high school. She could be married. I don't know. I should have asked my parents when I went to see them. It just slipped my mind. The middle girl is named Iva. I heard she got married, and I didn't even get an invitation."

Alex squeezed her hand, "That's sad. Family's really important. They're the only ones who love you unconditionally."

Mary reached for his other hand, not letting go of the one she held earlier, "I don't think that's true. I feel that way about you. There's so much I don't know about you, but if I never find out what happened to you in the ten years you can't remember, I will still care deeply."

"You know, I have to be nearly ten years older than you. Are you sure that won't make a difference?" he looked into her eyes and noticed they were moist. "You're not crying, are you?"

"Can you cry because you're happy? If you can, then that explains why I'm crying."

Alex put his hands on her shoulders, and Mary thought he was going to push her away again, but he did just the opposite. He bent down, pulling her slightly toward him, and brushed her lips with his. She pushed her mouth against his, opening her lips to his kiss. He reached behind her, finding her slim waist, and pulled her tightly against his body so that they were touching almost head to toe.

The kiss lasted long after propriety dictated a first kiss should end. She could feel any resistance being drained from her, and all she could think about was, *this beautiful man is going to make love to me.*

Alex wanted to take her to bed, but he hesitated. This was not some one-night stand. He cared for her. He wanted it to be right. So he stepped back.

Mary looked at him, a hurt look on her face. She thought in that instant he didn't want her. "Did I do something wrong?" she asked.

"Just the opposite. I want you, Mary. I'm shaking because of it. But I need to know it's the right thing for you, too."

"Oh yes, it is so right. I've never felt like this before. I tremble at your touch, even though I'm trying to be demure and compose myself," she reached for him.

"No, wait. I need to tell you something first," he had remembered about his marital situation after Mary's presence had short-circuited his clear thinking.

"Nothing could make any difference for me. I've had a lot of time to think about it. I'll take you no matter what."

"That's not fair. As long as you think I'm married, there would be a barrier between us, and I don't want that. I found out my wife is dead." There, it was out. No more reason to hold back.

Mary stepped back again, "When did you learn this?"

"After I left you the last time. When you apparently went home, I talked to a neighbor who knew her, and I verified it with the super of the building."

Mary didn't know what to say. There was nothing to stand between them now. And then she remembered. There were the ten years he couldn't account for, and the threat of

175

a firing squad or hanging. Still, she felt relieved. That had always been there, and she fell in love with him anyway.

Trying to get the mood back, she asked, "Dance with me?"

"There's no music."

"We can fix that," she answered with a seductive look. She walked across the room to the record player. She loaded a Patti Paige ballad and a couple of others and then strolled back to Alex, her arms out. He came willingly.

Neither of them heard the words, and when the first piece ended, they stood there waiting for the next song to drop down to the turntable. They stared into each other's eyes as Jo Stafford began to sing *You Belong To Me*. They moved even closer to one another. Their feet didn't move, and they swayed, both knowing the music was only the vessel to excuse their closeness. He kissed her long and deep, both their mouths opening to each other. Only then did he pick her up and carry her into the bedroom, the kiss continuing.

They slept till noon, but that was understandable. Neither of them fell asleep until well after midnight, as they consummated their love over and over.

Mary was the first to awaken. She silently crawled out of bed, finding her panties on the floor next to the side she'd ended up on. It wasn't cold in the apartment so she didn't bother dressing as she went to the kitchen. She wanted to prepare a gourmet breakfast for her lover, but she had no idea what he liked. She took a chance and made a bacon, cheese, and egg omelet, after putting the coffee on. When it perked, Alex stirred. "Oh, that smells good. So does the coffee."

She laughed, "Good morning, my love. Are you hungry?"

"Do you mean for food? I'm starved for that too."

"You really are a rake, aren't you?"

"If I am, you made me that way. Come back to bed. The food can wait."

"But it's all ready. I can't imagine you want to do something else but eat."

"That's because all you see is me. What I see is you."

"Come on. We have all the time in the world. This breakfast will spoil before we tire of each other."

Alex rolled out of bed, "You've got a point."

After breakfast, of which he approved heartily, she asked, "What would you like to do today, darling?"

He glanced toward the bedroom, and she said, "Oh no, you don't. If we go back in there, we'll never come out."

"Would that be so bad?" he was serious.

"No. But I'm hoping we'll have the rest of our lives to explore each other's bodies. We don't need to rush it."

"We got a good start last night," he said, remembering.

There was something unsaid between them. Alex had the feeling she wanted him to ask her to marry him. He wanted to do just that, but the ten years stopped him. He needed to find out where he'd been. Until he did, he didn't feel he had the right to make plans and involve Mary, even though he was sure he was in love.

At that moment, a thought entered the mind of the young, content lover. He had to talk to the detective.

38

Jim Denton was duly impressed with Vince Arrizano's complex. Even so, he couldn't wait to get out of there. He was thinking the guy must be really lonely. On the trip over, he wouldn't shut up. He even told him about the indictment he was under. Denton couldn't understand why he was so calm. He would probably go to prison. Arrizano just appeared to take it all in stride, though.

The trip back to the Alliant Arms went faster, or so it seemed. Denton supposed it was because the conversation on the way over was boring, although he was surprised by the revelation of the indictment against the gangster. He thought Vince Arrizano was untouchable since he'd probably bought off more than half the police force. This was the Feds, though. The assassination attempt, on the other hand, was no surprise, since the guy on top always has enemies who want to take over his share or have a grudge from when he himself climbed to the top of the ladder. Now it became even more likely he would be hit, because, with the indictment hanging over him, his cronies might worry he would rat on them to cut a deal with the authorities.

When he arrived back at the apartments, he decided to change clothes before going out to dinner. He thought about asking Mary Abrams to go with him. After changing to more casual attire, he wandered down the hall to Mary's place. When he knocked, there was no answer. *Oh well*, he thought, *maybe tomorrow*. He still needed to find a way to get that uniform out of her closet.

After a really filling Italian meal of lasagna with an antipasto, he went back to his apartment and promptly fell asleep. Around midnight, he moved from his couch to the bedroom.

After a boring day at the office, he again decided to ask Mary out to dinner. He'd left a little earlier than usual because there was nothing going on at work. He arrived at Mary's door just before two. He really expected her to be at work, but he knocked just in case, thinking if no one was there, he might jimmy the lock and get that uniform.

He was surprised to see Joe Chester. He had the impression the two were fighting since the Marine hadn't stayed there overnight the past few days. The thought occurred to the detective it might be harder to get in to steal the uniform with him there.

"Just the man I want to see," Alex said when he saw who was at the door.

Denton was surprised, "Why do you want to see me?"

"I've got a proposition for you."

"I'll bite. What is it?"

"You're a private investigator, right?"

"Yeah. Why?" he glanced inside the apartment, but he didn't see Mary.

"I need you to find somebody for me."

"I'm pretty expensive. Sure you can afford me?"

Now Alex was going to spring his idea, "You like Judy Graves, right?"

"Sure, but I don't think she feels the same." If he couldn't get together with Mary, as it now appeared, second best wasn't bad.

"What if I give you clear sailing with her, and you do me this favor? I'll even put in a good word for you," Alex was hoping he didn't find out about his relationship with Mary, and besides, it was the only thing he had to trade. He didn't think Denton would help him for free.

"I thought you were interested in Mary."

"Well, I am, but Judy seems to like me, so if I step out of the way with her, you'll have no competition. I happen to know she likes you too," he was stretching the truth a little, but all's fair in love and war.

Denton had decided to help anyway. He just wondered how far the man he knew as Joe Chester would go. "Who do you want me to find?"

"A woman named Gloria O'Bannion. She might be married by now. She was born in 1930, so she's 22 now. She lived here in 1942, but I lost track of her."

"You mean she lived at the Alliant Arms, or just in Chicago?"

"In these apartments. In the room Mary has now, as a matter of fact."

"What's your relationship with this woman?"

Alex knew that question was coming, and he was sure he would have to tell Denton everything. He took a deep breath.

Just then, Mary appeared, fully dressed, except for shoes. "He wants to find her for me. I found something when I moved in that belongs to her, that she left here. I think it might be important."

"What is it?"

"I'm sorry. It's a private thing, kind of in the female genre. It would be embarrassing to reveal it."

"Okay," Denton answered. "I'll see what I can find out. You look kind of dressed up. Are you guys going out?"

Mary answered before Alex could speak, "We're going out to dinner. Would you like to join us?" She crossed her fingers that he would say no. She wanted to be alone with Alex. She was disappointed when Denton answered in the affirmative.

This was all news to Alex, but he just went along with the charade. It was only about 2 pm in the afternoon, but they could eat early. There was no law against it.

It was a little after 3 pm when they walked into the downtown restaurant Jim Denton had suggested. He had driven since he knew where they were going. It was only two blocks from his office, and he said they served a really good open-faced prime rib sandwich, among other things.

The restaurant was nearly empty. There was a party of five seated in the main dining room; otherwise, they had the place to themselves. They were able to get a table looking out on the street, so they could people watch if they wanted.

It seemed a little early for alcohol to Alex and Mary, but Jim ordered a Manhattan. When his drink and their water arrived, they were ready to order. Alex took Jim's advice and ordered the prime rib, while Mary just wanted soup. Both men objected, saying she needed something more, but she held fast, professing she had to watch her figure. Jim made a joke about watching it for her, and they gratuitously laughed. Alex and Mary held hands under the table. Jim didn't appear to notice, as he watched people walk by outside.

When their food came, the men attacked it with a vengeance, while Mary toyed with her soup, stirring it, lifting a spoonful, and letting it drop back into the bowl. She really didn't appear to be hungry. Of course, it hadn't been that long ago she and Alex had eaten a huge breakfast.

They were about halfway through dinner when there was a commotion at the other occupied table across the room. A woman yelled out, "He can't breathe! Someone, please help!" The people at that table seemed to just stand there. They had at least gotten up.

Of their party, Alex was the closest to the others. He jumped up, his chair clattering to the restaurant floor. He ran to the man in obvious distress, who seemed to be choking. Alex moved behind him and, wrapping his arms around the rather large man, he clasped his hands just under the fellow's sternum. He yanked up violently, and a piece of meat that could have been steak flew out of the now breathing man's mouth.

Of course, they all thanked Alex profusely for acting so quickly and knowing what would dislodge the obstruction. Mary asked how he knew what to do, and Alex just shrugged his shoulders, and answered, "I don't know. It just seemed like it might work."

Jim patted him on the back and said, "Right man, right time. Good job." Alex himself was silently surprised he knew what to do.

The rest of their time there was uneventful. When the other people were finished and had paid, they all came over to see Alex and congratulate him again for saving their friend.

39

When he met with the others in the expedition, Oliver West told them about his experience in the restaurant and talking with the Japanese waiter, who hid the fact he spoke their language well. He'd already made up his mind to follow up on it, and he was encouraged to do so by the group. They in turn were going to check names on the crosses at the cemetery with their list of men missing in action.

The next day, he rose early and, after showering and dressing, he headed for the restaurant. He wore his uniform to look more official.

Before he was seated, he inquired about Shigera's hours, learning the man had the day off. He made an excuse that he had hired the man to show him around the island, but had forgotten to obtain his address; the counter woman was happy to supply it.

He was able to rent an old Jeep from the war at a place in downtown Honiara. Shigera's house was a little too far out of town to walk.

It was about 10 am when he arrived at the house, which was little more than a shack, and would probably blow away with a typhoon, but so far, it was still standing.

He'd just exited from the Jeep when a man he recognized as his waiter from the day before came out to meet him.

"What you want?" the man asked warily, as he recognized West.

"I came to find out why you put on that act back at the restaurant after I found out you speak English as well as I."

"It's just for the tourists. I don't mean any harm by it." West was impressed by the man's perfect speech and intonation.

"Look Kyoto, do you mind if I call you that?" and he continued before the little Japanese man could answer. "I'm looking for information about what happened to a man under my command during the war. I have a feeling you might know something about it, having been there yourself."

Shigera's face took on a defeated look, "I always dreaded that someone would come asking about that day. It's why I never went back to Japan."

"What do you mean?"

"I was a bad soldier. My superiors would never understand why I did what I did."

"What did you do?" West felt an old excitement. He knew he was closer to learning the truth of what happened that day so long ago, and why.

Jim Denton wasted no time in learning the address of Gloria O'Bannion Windsor. He had canvassed a few neighbors on that floor of the Alliant Arms and found out she had gotten married. Then he went to the Hall of Records in Chicago, where he learned her married name. It was easy after that to check on the change of addresses. She had filed one when they moved to San Diego. He relayed that information to Alex.

The next day, when he knew Mary was at work, and Alex had told him he was going down to the YMCA to retrieve clothes from a locker, Denton went down the hall to Mary's apartment. He knocked, and when no one answered, he used a piece of plastic to open the door by jamming it in behind the locking device, then forcing it to move back just enough so the door swung free. He looked around down the hall and, seeing no one, he entered Mary's apartment.

He went straight for the closet. When he opened the door to the storage space, it was empty, except for some women's clothes. Panicking, he could see his plan falling apart. Before he left, he decided to check other spaces. When he looked under Mary's bed, he found what he was looking for. He decided to take the entire uniform, including the helmet.

Peering out into the hall, he saw it was still empty, so he quickly went to his own apartment. Once there, he hid the telltale uniform in his own closet, and went to his refrigerator, got a beer, and sat down in his living room chair, heaving a sigh of relief.

Alex decided to visit Blake Evans in the hospital before returning to Mary's apartment. She wouldn't be home till around 5 pm, anyway. He timed his visit just right, arriving at the beginning of visiting hours.

The reporter was glad to see Alex. He hadn't had a visitor for more than a day. He had gotten his voice back by that morning. They talked for over an hour. Alex asked how his neck was feeling, and Blake told him it was healing so well, he might be released the next day. Alex also told him he was going to ask Mary to be his wife. Since Alex had saved his life, they were becoming great friends. Blake was happy for him. Then Alex said something that seemed out of place, even cryptic.

"If anything happens to me, would you look after Mary?"

Of course, Blake had answered, "Nothing's going to happen to you. You're going to live forever."

"Sure I am."

Blake Evans was going through a catharsis. He finally got it. He'd been going through life thinking everyone else inhabited the planet just for him, to give him everything he wanted. Now, after lying there watching others diligently trying to save him, when he thought he might die, it was suddenly clear to him. He was just one of many, and in a way, everyone was put on earth to make it work for each other. He didn't know it at the time, but the realization would actually give him a chance for a better life.

Jim Denton couldn't wait to take the uniform he'd stolen from Mary Abrams' apartment to the FBI office in Chicago. He called first for an appointment, and when the agent asked what it was about, he stated, "I have some information about an AWOL Marine." He was told to come in right away.

When he walked into the office, an agent, who identified himself as Special Agent Wilkins, led him to a cubicle in the back of the room.

"Now, what's this all about?" the agent began.

Denton didn't want to implicate Mary, so he said, "I met a man who was wearing the uniform of a Marine, but now he's masquerading as a civilian. I have the uniform in my car as proof."

"Bring it in and we'll have a look," the agent named Wilkins answered.

When Denton returned, he was carrying what he'd taken from Mary's apartment.

"That's an old fighting outfit from World War Two. Are you sure he didn't just get it from a costume place?"

That had never occurred to Jim Denton. He didn't know how to answer. Could it be that Joe Chester was a phony just trying to impress a beautiful woman?

When he didn't answer right away, Wilkins told him, "We'll look into it. Where can we find this AWOL Marine?"

Oliver West was a passenger in the Jeep he'd rented as Kyoto Shigera drove into the jungle north of town. He felt a sense of Déjà vu as they passed the airfield which was the scene of a fierce battle that had claimed many lives on both sides of the conflict; brave lives that were advancing their country's philosophy. They weren't involved in policymaking but were willing to lay down their lives for the cause.

Kyoto had told West an incredible story. He had been sent into the jungle to be a sniper. He had shown his superiors he was a good shot while taking target practice in Japan before being deployed to Guadalcanal. Then, his job was to kill as many of the enemy as he could. He had enough ammunition to wipe out a platoon of advancing enemy soldiers.

He climbed a palm tree and waited. He had time to think about what had led him there. He thought of himself as an

American. He'd only gone back to Japan because his father had demanded it. He was going to enroll at UCLA. He'd become a devout Baptist, and as a result, he was a pacifist. He had no desire to kill another human being, least of all one whom he considered his countryman.

Yet here he was, ready to do just that. He made up his mind, sitting there in that perch, to desert. He had fallen in love with a Polynesian girl named Meleia. He had finally outgrown his infatuation for the girl named Janet, who was far away in the land of the soldiers sent to take the island paradise. He wanted to marry and settle down, never to return to Japan or the United States.

On the fateful day, he had climbed down from the tree, ready to return to the village, when he saw a Marine, not 30 feet from where he stood. The Marine noticed Kyoto at the same instant. Strangely, the Marine did not immediately raise his rifle. Kyoto waited, unwilling to fire himself. Then the American did lift his weapon, but he hesitated. Kyoto fired first in self-defense, striking the Marine in his chest. He dropped his rifle and fell to the ground. As Kyoto reached him, the Marine died.

He was grief-stricken. He couldn't just leave the man there at the mercy of the animals of the jungle. He deserved a proper burial according to his faith. Kyoto dug a shallow grave, and after removing the dead man's dog tags, and placing the body in the hole, he covered it with dirt and palm fronds.

Kyoto, who had an American nickname of Willie handed Oliver West the dog tags of Alex O'Bannion. The major marked the grave they'd found so that he might be able to return and remove the body. He'd considered the

189

Marine named O'Bannion his friend, in spite of the difference in their ranks, and he wanted to give him a proper burial, hopefully at Arlington in the United States. Of course, that would be up to higher authorities.

After returning to Kyoto's home, Oliver and his unlikely new friend uncharacteristically hugged before parting.

40

The remains of Private Alex O'Bannion of the United States Marine Corps were flown into Andrews Air Force Base in Washington, D.C. on November 23rd, 1952, ten and a half years after he died defending his country and avenging Pearl Harbor. From there, they were taken to Arlington National Cemetery for burial. A brief ceremony preceded the interment. Surviving members of his squad were the only ones in attendance. Oliver West had paid their expenses. An early winter storm was expected the next day, but on this afternoon, it was bright, sunny, and 65 degrees.

There were others who might have attended the burial, but they had not been informed it was taking place; people from Chicago who owed their lives, or their happiness, to a man they knew as either Alex O'Bannion or Joe Chester.

Blake Evans was released from the hospital on that day. Outside, the city had hunkered down for the early winter storm that blew in from the northwest and blanketed the streets with a thin layer of snow.

No one had come to take Blake home. Alex O'Bannion would most certainly have been there, but no one had seen the man they knew as Joe Chester for nearly three months. So Blake caught a cab to take him to the *Chicago Sun*

Express building. There was nothing waiting for him at his apartment. He had no wife or girlfriend. He had a big story to write…but he didn't know all of it yet.

A few miles south, at the Alliant Arms, on the second floor to be specific, things had changed dramatically from a few months earlier. Judy Graves, on learning that her father would most likely be going to prison, had a change of heart. She changed her name back to Arrizano, much to her dad's pleasure. She hadn't moved out of her apartment yet, but she intended to move back to the beachfront property, so she could look after it while Vince was away. They had an understanding that he would divest himself of all criminal activity, and become a model citizen when he was released.

Jim Denton had made a fool of himself. The FBI had not found any clues as to who owned the old Marine Corps uniform, and they had returned it to Denton. By that time, Alex or Joe was nowhere to be found. Denton stuffed the uniform back under his bed, to be out of the way until he could find a way to sneak it back to Mary Abrams' closet. When he felt he could return it, he looked under his bed, and it had mysteriously disappeared—helmet and all.

Mary Abrams was heartbroken. She had somehow lost the love of her life, and she didn't understand. She had no way of knowing the answer would come to her in another month. The uniform was gone from her closet, and Alex had disappeared without a trace. It made no sense.

They had that one night, and he was happy. She knew it. She could feel that he wanted to ask her to marry him, and she would have screamed yes! There was no indication when he left that day that she would never see him again.

She quit her job and returned to her family's home. Even there, no one could bring her out of her malaise.

It wasn't until she began having morning sickness that she knew she was going to have Alex's baby. It would be a part of him. She wouldn't be alone. She began to feel life had some meaning for her, after all. She was sure Alex would not have left her of his own free will. He wasn't that type at all.

Mary wouldn't tell her parents who the father was when they became aware, she was to have a baby. They couldn't fathom that she wanted to raise the child on her own. Adoption was the only answer to their minds. Even her father took her mother's side. It became so unbearable for her that she had to get away from their constant pounding about her situation. She moved back to Chicago, and the Alliant Arms. She had a little money left that she had saved.

It had been an improbable romance, hers and Alex's. She was a Jew, though not a practicing one, and he was a Gentile. They had been together such a short time, not long enough to know each other. Still, the flame of passion had burned bright between them as they realized how they felt. That flame had flickered in her heart when he disappeared, but it wasn't extinguished, and maybe it never would be, now that she had something of him to hold on to. He had taught her what love is, and she would never forget.

One day late in November, after Mary had returned to Chicago, Blake Evans came to call. He was still working on his exclusive about the man he knew as Joe Chester. He knew about the rescue of Judy Graves, of course, and the fact that he himself was probably still alive because of Joe's involvement. While he'd been in the hospital, the story broke about the attempt on the life of Vince Arrizano, and the part a man named Joe Chester had in saving him. He hadn't heard about the chance meeting with the stranger in the restaurant that had resulted in yet another life being saved. That tidbit would be related by a pretty redhead named Mary Abrams.

The promise of a blockbuster article was hanging over him. His editor had given him a deadline, which was extended because Blake had been almost killed. Now that the reporter was completely recovered, the deadline was reinstated. If the young reporter didn't have a completed story on the editor's desk by the 1st of December, it would not only be killed, but Blake would lose his job, which had been precarious from the beginning. That's why he was glad when he heard Mary had moved back into the Alliant Arms. She should be able to help him complete the piece.

Blake had a hard time when Mary was in the room. He tried to be analytic and cool, but there was an attraction he'd never admitted to anyone, especially her. He was not the smoothest Romeo when it came to women, though he had thought otherwise.

He was 25 years and 10 days old if one were counting. He'd had exactly two girlfriends in his young existence if you count the one when he was 11. He always thought before that it was their shortcoming that they weren't interested.

He knew Joe Chester had disappeared, and that Mary had feelings for him. Perhaps he would return, but maybe not. There was something about the man that didn't ring true, like the lie about where he came from. Still, he had shown compassion where Blake was concerned by checking up on him, and really, saving his life. He'd also confided how he felt about Mary. That's another reason his disappearance made no sense.

Blake wished he could summon enough courage to ask Mary on a date. But for now, he had to be an investigative reporter. His job depended upon it.

He purposely waited until 6 pm in the evening to call on her, thinking she probably worked that day. When he knocked on her door, he heard her yell, "Just a minute!"

When she opened the door and saw Blake standing there, she smiled, "Mister Evans, I presume. What brings you to my door?" Then she added, "I'm sorry it took me so long to answer. I was just putting something in the oven."

"That's all right Mary, but please, call me Blake." He just stood there, taking her in. She was wearing an apron over what he assumed were her work clothes. She was barefoot, so she was much shorter than him. That didn't detract from his attraction. "I'm still working on the story from before, and I had a few questions for you if you don't mind," he continued.

Mary got a wistful look, but she said, "No, I don't mind. Come in, won't you? I have lasagna in the oven that'll be ready in about 40 minutes. Won't you join me for dinner?"

It was a dream come true for the shy reporter. "That would be great. I haven't eaten yet, and that really smells good," he said, as he pointed toward the kitchen.

"We'll see if it's any good. I haven't tried this recipe before."

Dinner was perfect, as far as Blake was concerned. Mary had made a green salad to go with the Italian food. She'd introduced him to blue cheese dressing that he liked.

They made very little conversation during the meal—just courteous stuff, like how was your day?

Mary had taken the apron off, and when she stood up to clear the table, Blake noticed that she'd gained some weight in a telltale place. He'd thought her face was a little fuller when he'd first seen her in the doorway.

They moved into the living room, and Blake took out a pad and pencil. When asked, Mary told him she didn't really know where the man he knew as Joe Chester had lived before coming to Chicago. She'd lied about him being her cousin, but Blake had already learned that. She did admit that the mystery man had shown up at her door looking for his family, and she'd felt sorry for him, and let him in to rest. She said she was attracted to him, so he'd stayed at her place with permission when she went to work. That's when he smelled the smoke from the fire at Judy Graves' apartment.

"Look, Mary, I don't know whether you're telling me the truth or not, but that's the way I'll write it. I don't want to cause you any grief."

Because she was grateful, she told him about what happened at the restaurant, and that the man had survived because of Joe's quick action. She still hesitated to give Alex's real name. She didn't really want to answer any more questions after that. It was a very painful subject for her.

Blake summoned up enough courage to ask one more question, "Would you consider having dinner with me?"

"We just ate," she gave the obvious answer, but she knew what he meant.

"No, tomorrow maybe," he blushed.

For some unknown reason, she liked Blake. It hadn't been that way at first. She'd thought him intrusive. That was natural because she had been forced to lie, which is never easy for most people.

"I'd love to," she answered, changing his blush to a smile of pleasure.

As they were waiting for their food to come, and sipping their Margaritas while sitting in the upscale restaurant where Blake had made reservations immediately after leaving Mary Abrams' apartment the night before, he asked her a pointed question. He didn't think she'd react angrily in the setting he had picked. "Are you going to have a baby, Mary?"

She was quiet, a look of surprise on her face. Then, she spoke, "How dare you ask me that! It's none of your business." Then she began to cry.

He immediately realized he'd made a mistake. Hurting her was the last thing he would do intentionally.

"I'm sorry, Mary. It's just that I want to help."

She regained some of her composure, "What can you do to help? No one can help me!"

"I could marry you!" There, it was out. He'd been thinking about it ever since he saw her the night before, and realized she was in trouble.

"What?"

"Look. I love children, and I've liked you since the first time I saw you. There's something else. It has nothing to do with how I feel about you, but you need to know. When Joe came to the hospital to visit me just before he disappeared, he asked me to watch after you if he couldn't. It was right after he told me he wanted to ask you to marry him."

With that pronouncement, Mary began to cry again.

Blake took her hand and continued, "I know I'm not the catch of the century, but I'd make you a good husband. If you say jump, I'll say how high, and assume the position."

She laughed at that. The gloomy spell was broken. "You are kind of good-looking," and she added, "in a spooky kind of way."

Since time was important, they visited the license bureau the next day. Woolworth's was happy to give her the afternoon off. Three days later, they were married, giving her unborn child a father and a name.

Post Mortem

It was a typical sunny afternoon at the Marine Corps Recruit Depot in San Diego, California when the brigade gathered on the parade grounds for the ceremony. As if on cue, and recognizing the significance of what was to come, the coastal marine layer low clouds had retreated over the Point Loma hills and offshore only an hour before.

Normally, chairs would be set up for military dignitaries to observe the troops as they passed by. On this occasion, however, civilians occupied the place of honor.

She would remember the date. It was December 30th, 1952. It should have been 1942, but better late than never, as they say. She sat there quietly, waiting for the words that had taken so long in coming.

She wasn't alone. Other guests had been flown in from Chicago. She didn't know them, but she was aware they had a stake in the final outcome that had its beginning long ago on the island of Guadalcanal, Solomon Islands, South Pacific.

She had sent a letter east to Chicago, and because of that, these other people had shown up. It was all very strange, but she was just following orders.

It began when she herself received a letter from her brother, Alex. It was undated, and had no return address. The oddest thing, however, was the fact there was no stamp on the envelope.

As she had read the letter, which was handwritten, she felt a chill, even though she sat in front of a warm fire emanating from her fireplace. It read:

Hi Sis,

I'll bet you're shocked, hearing from me after all this time. I just want you to know I miss you very much. I wish I could have seen you one more time. I learned where you live just yesterday. That's why this letter is so late in coming.

If you decide to have some kind of service, there are some people I'd like for you to invite. They live in Chicago so I'm not sure if they'll show up, but I wouldn't want to leave them out since they have been very kind to me, even though I was a stranger to them.

Don't worry about me. I am at peace.

The letter went on to list the names of those he wanted to attend and was signed, "Your loving brother, Alex."

The very next day, she received another letter, informing her about the military ceremony in honor of her brother. So here she was.

At the end of the single row of chairs sat a Japanese gentleman. He was not with the group from the Midwest. She had no idea why he was there. He too was a civilian. Had the ceremony taken place long ago, he most certainly would not have been allowed to attend.

A man in uniform she identified as a colonel by the insignia on his collars stood behind a desk, adjusted a microphone, and faced the gathered troops, who had come to attention.

"This ceremony is very late in coming. The young man we are here to honor on this day was a brave Marine who gave his life in the service of his country. Had he lived to fulfill the promise of his enlistment, we might have offered a higher salute to his bravery. As it is, we are gathered here to witness the presentation of the Purple Heart for wounds suffered on the battlefield." With that proclamation, the colonel stepped away from the podium and moved down the row of people till he stood in front of the young woman.

He then continued, "I humbly present this Purple Heart to you, Mrs. Gloria O'Bannion Windsor," as he placed the ribboned medal over her head and around her neck, "with the deepest appreciation for the service and sacrifice of your brother, Private Alex O'Bannion to the Marine Corps of the United States of America and the country for which we all serve." He reached down and hugged the outwardly sobbing woman and saluted, before returning to the podium to dismiss the troops.

All the other guests stood and clapped. The colonel who had presented the medal was Oliver West. Standing next to Alex's sister was Mary Abrams Evans and her husband Blake, Vince Arrizano and his daughter Judy, Sergeant Bill Helmand, and the little Japanese man, whose name was Kyoto Shigera.

Later, on the way back to their parked cars, Gloria sought out Mary Evans. "We've never met, but I'm the one who sent you the letter letting you know about this ceremony."

Mary took her hand, "I know. I'm so glad to meet you. I just wish the circumstances were more pleasant, and Alex was here too."

"How do you know my brother? Did I just forget you when I lived in Chicago growing up?" Gloria had a confused look.

Mary was sure there was no way she could make this woman understand, so she simply answered, "We were old friends."

Gloria noticed she was in a family way and asked, "When is the baby due?"

The visibly pregnant woman answered, "Mid-summer."

"Do you have a name picked out?"

Mary didn't hesitate, "We want to name him Alex if it's a boy, and Alexa if it's a girl. I hope you don't mind."

"I'd be honored. I'm sure my brother would be too." Then, she again asked, "How did you know my brother? You couldn't have been much more than ten when he died."

Mary smiled, "Oh, I was a little older than that and very wise for my age."

As they were leaving the parade grounds, Blake asked Mary, "What did you think?"

Rather than answer the way her husband expected, she took his hand and said, "I'd like to think that somewhere out there, is a gentleman by the name of Joe Chester, that our son or daughter might someday meet."

The End